The Cursed Hollow

Return to Sleepy Hollow, Part 1

Candace Wondrak

Chapter One – Kat

Out of all the reasons for me to come back to this miserable, boring, quaint town, I never thought it would be because of my dad's death. Like all kids, I assumed my parents would stick around for a long while yet, even though they were divorced and on different sides of the globe. Yes, at twenty-four years old, I was back for the absolute worst reason possible.

The town, on maps, was technically called Tarry, but everyone always called it by its spookier, folktale-esque name.

Sleepy Hollow.

Yeah, *that* Sleepy Hollow. Headless Horseman, Ichabod Crane, and all that shit. My dad loved it. It's why he wanted to move there, why my parents got divorced. His obsession drove Mom away, and she took me with her. I did spend far too much time in Sleepy Hollow myself, however. My summers growing up were spent wandering the cemeteries and going to all their festivals and outdoor get-togethers.

You'd be surprised how many people in Sleepy Hollow believed in the stories. Personally, I found them ridiculous, because they were written by some guy while he was abroad. Sure, he might've based some of the details off of things that actually happened, but a headless dude roaming around in search of his head? Don't make me laugh.

And don't get me started on my name, either. I went by Kat, but that's only because my full name reminded me of my dad, which in turn reminded me of his obsession. I was their only child, and, shocker, Dad had begged my mom to name me after the famous chick in the stories. My full name was Katrina.

I sat in the backseat of the Uber, watching as the houses rolled by. I held my phone against my ears, listening to my mom talk, "I'm sorry I couldn't make it, honey. If I could've dropped everything and flew back into the States, I would've." Mom was currently off in India or some other country, doing whatever it was she did. Collecting art? Buying art? Something important and useless, all the same.

"It's okay. I'm just going to have a look at his will, see how he wanted to be taken care of, and then…" I trailed off. "Then pack up the house, I guess. Put it on the market."

"That's a good idea. I'm sure he left everything to you. You can pay off your loans with that money."

Oh, yeah. What a bright side to look at there. My dad died, so I got to pay off my student loans years ahead of time. Whoo-hoo.

The Uber pulled to a stop before the address I'd given him. "I'm here. I'll text you later." After saying my goodbyes and hanging up, I tipped the driver and got out, moving to get my luggage from the back. I'd guessed I'd be here for a week, maybe two, depending on the arrangements he wanted and how much crap he had packed away in the house.

As I shut the trunk, the driver poked his head out of the window. "Remember, don't cross the bridge at midnight." With a smile and a wave, he was off, driving away and leaving me with a bad taste in my mouth.

Don't cross the bridge at midnight. What did I look like, a newbie? Of course I wouldn't cross the bridge at midnight, mostly because someone would inevitably see me doing it and then start to spread rumors that I was cursed. This town and its damned ghost stories; I'd rather avoid it all entirely.

Heaving a sigh, I turned to the house. Beyond a short, black iron fence sat a two-story house. Its siding was painted a dark grey, the trim a bright white. Gables and arches; it was a beautiful home, well taken care of, gothic in design. If I wasn't so against this town, I would think about moving here and taking the house as my own. It wasn't like I had a great job back home. I rented a studio apartment and worked as a retail associate. That lovely college degree hard at work.

I closed my eyes for a moment, feeling the breeze whip through my brown hair. The weather was never too hot here, even in the summertime. It was either somewhat chilly or perfectly pleasant, the kind of weather you could wear a light jacket in and not sweat.

Once I'd gathered up my courage, I headed past the wrought iron gates and headed to the front porch. I set my luggage down and went to the rock I knew held a key. It was so obviously fake too, not even matching the color of the rocks it was around.

I walked inside the house, dropping my luggage at the base of the stairs. I knew he had a room for me, even though I'd stopped coming during the summer after I'd turned eighteen. I hadn't seen or talked to my dad in years. I wanted to forget about him like Mom did.

That sounded bad, but I swear, he was obsessed with the legends surrounding Sleepy Hollow. It was all he talked about. My dad practically breathed Sleepy Hollow, and I was sure he dreamt about it, too.

Annoying. There was no other word for it.

I checked the house. Everything looked untouched, messy in the way I knew he liked. Dishes were piled up in the sink, the trash can full and smelly. The living room held a couch, a table, and a TV. It was where he ate his meals and watched his favorite sitcoms—the few hours of the day when he wasn't drowning himself in his work.

Setting my hand on the trim around the archway that connected the living room to the hallway near the stairs, I sighed. This definitely wasn't what I wanted to be doing. None of this was going to be fun.

Pushing off the wall, I grabbed my luggage and headed up the stairs. I went straight past my dad's room—that would be the last room I went through, purely because I knew everything in it he loved, from his worn, stained shirts to his magic 8 ball which he refused to get rid of, even though it had lost a lot of the liquid inside it. My childhood room, the room I crashed in during summers growing up, was right beside his. His office and the bathroom were on the opposite side of the second floor.

My room was mostly bare, save for a few stuffed animals I'd won at the numerous carnivals this place had during the summer. The walls were a boring white, no wallpaper, nothing hanging on them. Nothing fancy, because even when I was younger, I hated being here. Sleepy Hollow was never my home; it was Dad's.

I sighed for about the millionth time today as I set my luggage on the foot of the twin bed, sitting beside it. I hadn't packed much, because I didn't want to be here for longer than I had to. Plus, the bills at home would only keep piling up. Since retail in America was such a lovely thing, I got no paid vacation time, no sick days, no personal days. All of this was unpaid. I was losing money to be here.

After sitting there in silence for a while, I dialed the number that had called me to tell me my dad had passed. His lawyer, Mike. He had Dad's will, and hopefully could help me figure out how to arrange a funeral and stuff. Being only twenty-four, I'd never even been to one before. The only funerals I'd seen were on TV and in the movies.

At least, I hoped he could. Maybe he would simply give me a copy of my dad's will and be off. I didn't know how these things worked.

Mike didn't pick up, so I let it go to voicemail. "Hey, Mike. It's Kat. I'm here, ready to meet whenever you are to go over the will. Give me a call back when you can, thanks." My thumb pressed the red button on the screen to end the call, and I heaved yet another sigh.

This place was going to be the death of me.

I got up, used the bathroom, and went back downstairs. I still wore my shoes, not knowing when the last time my dad had actually cleaned his house. His nose was always so deep in books that he forgot to bathe.

Yeah, ew.

I wandered in the kitchen, peeking in the fridge. I kept the lights off, for there was plenty of daylight streaming in through the windows. He had a bit of food, but not much. I'd probably have to make a run to the store, or do a lot of eating out. The diners here did have good food…

The sounds of a key sliding into a lock alerted me to someone else's presence. I quietly closed the fridge, waiting as I heard the front door to the house open. Someone was here, but who? They might've had a key, but I wasn't aware of anyone who knew my dad well enough to have a key to his damn house.

I grabbed the nearest thing to me—the dirty frying pan on top of the dishes in the sink, tiptoeing quietly to the end of the kitchen. Footsteps headed up the stairs, apparently knowing precisely where to go.

My teeth ground as I trailed after him. I found him in my dad's office, bent over and digging through the drawers in his desk. Lifting the frying pan, I said, "Who the fuck are you?" He seemed thin enough; I could probably take his ass from here to the damned bridge no one wanted to cross at midnight if I tried.

The man jerked up, nearly tripping over his own feet when he saw me. Behind his thin-rimmed glasses, I realized he wasn't that much older than me. Maybe thirty, at the most. He was at least a foot taller than me, but that wasn't hard to do because I was so short. His slender frame wore a button-down shirt tucked into a pair of dress pants.

He wasn't exactly what I would imagine if I pictured an intruder or a thief. Then again, he did have a key to the house, so he must've known my dad. My dad must've trusted him. Personally, I'd never seen the guy before, so I wasn't sure whether to hit him with the dirty frying pan or not.

I was leaning toward the former, especially since he wasn't answering me.

"I said," I spoke, over-enunciating my words to make sure he understood them, "who the fuck are you?" My fingers gripped the frying pan's handle tighter. He might've been kind of cute, but I was not above whooping some cute ass.

"I worked with your father," he quickly said, extending his hand to me. "Or I did, before he…" He quieted, genuine sorrow flashing in his green eyes, eyes a similar color to mine. The man bent his head, his wavy brown hair falling over his forehead. "I'm sorry. I didn't know anyone was here. I didn't think…well, I didn't think anyone would come."

"I'm his daughter," I replied, glaring.

"Yes, he did mention you often, but I…well, you never came." It sounded almost like this guy was judging me. Who the hell did he think he was?

"I came here during the summers growing up, and not once did I ever meet you," I growled out. This guy might look like the nerdy, cute type, but he had insulting someone down pat.

He blinked, his back straightening. His jaw was thin, angular. If he was a few shades paler, I would've called him a vampire. A shame I used to love those pale, blood-sucking guys in the movies. "Your father found me a few years ago…I'm sorry. Were you about to hit me with that frying pan?"

I met his incredulous and slightly worried stare. "I'm still thinking about it, honestly."

The man shut the drawer he'd been searching in, giving me a tiny smile. "Why don't we go downstairs and talk? I can make us some tea."

What a nice and disgusting offer, for someone who was trespassing on my dead dad's property. I mean, just because he had a key didn't mean he was welcome to waltz in whenever he wanted, right? And with my dad dead, this house was mine anyway. I didn't know this guy. He could be a serial killer for all I knew.

"Maybe after we talk, you can finally set down that pan," he added, obviously uneasy.

I stepped aside, letting him out of the office. As he went down the stairs, I threw a look around the room. Even though I hated my dad's obsession with Sleepy Hollow, it didn't feel right to let someone dig through his stuff like that. How was I to know whether or not this guy even knew my dad? Maybe he stole those keys. Maybe he was a liar.

I kept the frying pan by my side as I followed him into the kitchen. He seemed to make himself right at home, telling me to sit in the living room while he made the tea. Maybe I'd seen too many movies, but all I could think was *poison*, so I declined. Instead, I stood there watching him.

Wait a minute. I wasn't even going to drink the damn tea, so all of my posturing was pointless. Apparently if you wanted a badass, you shouldn't come to me.

Soon enough, we were in the living room, my frying pan on my knees, the tea the man had made me sitting on the coffee table before me. He sipped from his own mug before meeting my eyes. The more I looked at him, the cuter he became.

I wanted to smack myself. Now was not the time to be checking out possible men to date. I was here to do my dad's final arrangements, nothing more.

"So who exactly are you?" I broke the silence of the room, watching as he shifted his weight and looked uneasy. He did not like questions about himself, did he? "You were working with my dad?" I chuckled. "I'm surprised he had money to pay you."

"Oh, he wasn't paying me, just like he wasn't paying the bills to live here. I was." When I glared at him, he quickly said, "But everything is in your father's name, so feel free to do whatever you want with it."

"What are you, some kind of Richie Rich?"

He sipped his tea again, his emerald eyes falling to the floor. "I do come from old money. It is how your father found me."

"He was looking for a sugar daddy?"

My words caused the man to blush. A thirty-year-old man was before me, sipping tea and blushing. What in the world... "He was looking for someone who believed him, in his work. When he showed me what he was working on, I had no choice but to join him."

"You still never told me your name."

"That is because I know you're not a fan of all of this. Sleepy Hollow, the legends."

The longer he stalled, the weirder this became. I only glared.

"My parents named me Irving, because there were already a dozen Ichabods in our family. I like to go by my last name, though." His lips parted slightly as he paused, as if I should already know what it was. And, I supposed I did. "Crane."

Irving Crane.

My heart felt...heavy, strange in my chest. The man before me was a Crane. Of course he was. This wouldn't be Sleepy Hollow if someone didn't have the last name of Crane.

I let out a laugh, but the laugh sounded fake, so I stopped it instantly. "I'm surprised my dad never tried to set us up. I'm named after—"

"I know," Crane said, touching the middle of his glasses to push them up farther. "Katrina Van Tassel, but your father always called you Kat. You do look like him, a bit. You also look like the paintings in town of Katrina. You'll be popular around here."

Ugh. Being popular for looking like a lady from an old urban legend was not on my list of things to do. "I'm not staying," I declared. "I only came to set up arrangements for him and to pack this stuff up."

"Right. Of course. Why would you stay?" Crane let out a sad smile, and even though we were strangers, I didn't like the expression on his face. He looked much better when he wasn't so damned sad. "Before his…death," he paused, letting the word sink in, "we were working on something very important. I was hoping to grab the research before…" Again, he stopped himself, almost like he didn't want me to know what he and my dad were doing.

It was stupid, but I was curious. What could my dad have spent his whole life working on? What was more important than staying married to my mom? So I asked quietly, "What were you working on?"

"I don't think you really would want to know," Crane said, setting his empty cup on the table.

I hated when people told me what I needed, what I thought, or what I wanted. No one was in my head but me. "I asked, didn't I?"

"Sleepy Hollow is not like anywhere else," Crane went on, looking uncomfortable. "The veil between earth and the otherworld is thin. It is remarkably easy to hold seances here—" At the words *otherworld* and *seances*, my blood grew hot and I frowned, which he didn't notice, for he went on, "And possessions are more frequent here than anywhere else. We were working on something to change that."

"Ghosts," I muttered the word. "You're talking about ghosts."

"I don't like to use that word, because not everything that lives in the otherworld is a ghost. *Spirit* is more well-suited—"

I stood, still holding onto the frying pan. "Get out."

"What?"

"Get out of this house," I said, using my frying pan to point towards the door.

"But I—"

I grabbed his arm, pushing him out of the living room and to the front door. "Keys," I demanded. Crane sputtered, and when he made no moves to get his keys, I turned my hand, reaching into his back pocket, grabbing them myself. I'd seen the indentation when he was making the tea.

"Kat, I—"

I heard no more, mostly because he'd stopped the moment I shoved him outside and slammed the door in his face. Holding the frying pan in one hand and his keys in the other, I leaned my back on the door and held in a groan.

Ghosts? Spirits? What in the world was my dad up to? I hated calling him crazy, but he was totally off his rocker. So was his best friend-slash-coworker-slash-sugar-daddy.

After a moment of silence, Crane knocked on the outside of the door, saying, "Uh, you took my car and house keys as well. You can keep your father's key, but can I at least have those back? I'd hate to have to walk home—"

Letting out an annoyed sound, I stuck the frying pan between my side and my armpit, fumbling with the keys to take the house key off. I yanked open the door, threw the rest of the keys at his chest, and slammed it again. This time it would stay shut.

No more talk of ghosts. Ghosts were not real.

Or spirits, or whatever.

I flipped the lock, peering out through the glass beside the door, watching as Crane walked away. He stepped off the porch, headed down the concrete path to the sidewalk, but he stopped halfway down, his shoulders tightening. Crane threw a look over his shoulder, as if getting one last look at the house before going. The bastard could look at it all he wanted; he just wasn't allowed inside.

I felt myself relax once he'd gotten into his car and drove away. "Ghosts," I muttered to myself, shaking my head. "Fucking ghosts." A loud noise came from upstairs, and I instantly turned my head towards the stairs. "What in the hell," I whispered, heading up.

The moment I reached the top of the stairs, my legs froze. A shiver swept over me as I stared at the old, yellowed globe laying in the center of the hallway, just outside the office's door, which was now closed.

I grabbed the globe, juggling both it and the frying pan in one hand while I opened the office door. Or tried to, at least. The door didn't budge; I jiggled the knob, leaned my whole body against the door—nothing.

Okay, I'd be the first to admit, this was a little creepy, but it definitely wasn't ghosts. Ghosts, spirits, whatever you wanted to call them, weren't real.

"What the hell," I muttered under my breath, releasing the knob, about ready to break down the door myself. I clenched my fingers into a fist before trying it one last time. This time, shocker, the door opened without a problem, but my relief was short-lived as my eyes scanned the room.

The room I was just in, the room I'd followed Crane out of. We'd been alone in it, and I remembered it being much cleaner before.

The office was a mess. Papers were scattered everywhere, all the drawers in the desk open, some of them on the floor. The books on the built-in bookcases were haphazardly tossed about. It was almost like a hurricane had whipped its way through here.

I spotted something even stranger than the rest of the messy room: the window was wide open, the curtains fluttering about in the wind. The window, I knew for a fact, hadn't been open before. I thought about going to close it, but it was clear someone had gotten in and out of the house quietly. I had to report this.

I did what any sane person would do after discovering a tossed room and a possible break-in. I called the cops.

Chapter Two

I sat on the steps of the porch, my phone in one hand, frying pan in the other as I waited for the police to get here. For a small town, they sure were slow. My eyes studied the bits of burnt food lining the inside of the pan, and I wondered if it was the last meal my dad ate before he died.

How disgusting was that?

After a while, red and blue flashing lights appeared before the house, and I looked up, getting to my feet as I watched the officer park his car and slowly get out. Just one cop for a break-in, huh? Whatever. Maybe this place didn't have cops to spare.

I met the officer halfway, about to greet him when I realized whose blonde head was attached to the dark blue uniform. It was a blonde head I recognized, one I hadn't seen in years. A blonde head I'd long forgotten about, mainly because I wanted to forget everything involving this place—until now, that was.

"Well, well, well, look who it is," the man spoke, an easy smile spreading on his face. Two deep dimples appeared on his cheeks, and I resisted my urge to touch them. I'd always been fascinated with his dimples, mostly because I didn't have them myself.

Oh, and also because I used to have the biggest crush on the man, although back then he was a boy. He was a boy, and I was a girl, and we spent most of our summertime together. At least until I turned eighteen and stopped coming because I was legally an adult and it became my choice.

His teeth were white and flawless, just as I remembered. He'd gotten braces when we were twelve, and ever since he sprouted up and starting gaining muscles, I'd had the hots for him. He was even wider than he was when we were young; I'd bet any money that if I tore off his clothes I'd see a six-pack on his abdomen. His blonde hair was cut short, an inch, maybe, slightly longer on top and trimmed shorter on the sides.

My lower stomach burned. Damn, I wanted to jump him, or climb him like a tree.

Brom Brunt, though everyone always called him Bones. It had taken a few years for me to get used to calling him Bones, but none of that mattered now. My dad had enjoyed watching us together, I think because it made him picture us as our namesakes.

Yes, just like that weirdo Crane, Bones was the other part of the love triangle of Sleepy Hollow.

For those of you who don't know the legend—here it is, short and quick: Ichabod Crane wanted to marry Katrina Van Tassel, mostly for her wealth since she was the last child of a wealthy farmer. A love triangle of sorts ensued between Ichabod and the local town hero, Abraham Van Brunt. In the end, Abraham married her, or so the story said. What really happened, how close to the truth it all was, was anyone's guess.

You might have noticed I kept out the most famous part of that whole story, and that's because I did it on purpose. You see, I'm not a huge fan of the Headless Horseman, mostly because most people nowadays believed the guy in the headless suit was just Abraham Van Brunt playing tricks on Ichabod Crane.

There was no Headless Horseman, just like there weren't ghosts.

"Kat Aleson, back in town," Bones spoke, grinning. "Never thought I'd see you again. Figured you'd forgotten about us."

I managed to shrug. Doing anything while under the intense and handsome blue stare Bones had was beyond difficult. "I wanted to, but here I am."

The smile on his face faltered, a solemn expression taking its place. "Here you are, but not for good reasons. I heard what happened to your dad. I'm sorry." His thumbs hooked on his belt, and his eyes lingered on me for a few minutes before turning to stare up at the house. "Now your call said there was a break-in?"

Good. Right to business. No more small talk, no reminiscing. I didn't want to talk about the old times either, as fun as spending time with Bones had been. We were both adults now, and I had no idea what kind of person he was today.

Sexy, definitely, but was he a good guy? You never could tell with people, especially the attractive ones. Their pretty faces often held equally as pretty lies.

"Yes," I said, leading him to the house. We stepped inside. "I was in the room just before, then I heard a loud noise and I went upstairs to check. I found my dad's globe on the floor and the door shut—which I didn't close."

As we headed up the stairs, Bones asked, "And what were you doing before you heard the noise?"

"I was downstairs, talking to…" I trailed off, picturing Crane's somewhat awkward demeanor. Had I really freaked him out so badly with my attitude and my frying pan, or was he in on it—distracting me while someone else went through my dad's office?

We stopped just outside the office door, which I left open. Bones's blue eyes studied me. "Talking to who?"

"Irving Crane," I said, noting the way Bones frowned at the mention of his name.

"What was he doing here, alone with you?" If a third-party outsider happened to hear his question, they might start to think he was jealous or something. That, or he really didn't like Crane.

My eyebrows furrowed. "He walked into the house like he owned the place, which maybe he does in a way, since apparently he was helping my dad pay the bills. He started going through the office, and then I caught him. We went downstairs, he made some tea, and he started talking about ghosts and shit, and then I kicked him out."

Bones started investigating the room, tossing a glance back at me. "And you didn't hear anyone else enter the house?"

"Nope. Just him, and it wasn't even two seconds after he was gone that I heard the noise and came back upstairs." I let out a loud breath, crossing my arms— kind of hard to do while holding the frying pan—as I leaned on the door frame. "I honestly don't know how this happened."

"Did you plan on attacking someone with that frying pan?"

"Joke all you want, but one whack with this on the back of your head, and you're out."

His blue eyes danced with laughter. "Know that from personal experience?" Bones chuckled to himself, his wide shoulders rising and falling, catching his snug uniform over his muscles. Suddenly I could not get the thought of him naked from my mind.

Hmm. Maybe it'd just been too long since I'd had sex.

"Uh" was my brilliant reply. I left him to put the pan in the kitchen, cursing myself for looking so dumb. Why didn't I set the pan down before he got here? Granted, I didn't know it'd be him who'd show up, I didn't even know Bones was a cop around here, but still. I felt stupid and silly.

By the time I was ready to return to the scene of the crime, Bones was walking down the stairs, meeting me before the front door. "I closed the window for you. I would clean those papers up, if I were you."

I gave him a weird look. "What are you talking about? Aren't you going to, I don't know, investigate?"

Bones sighed. Not once in my life had I ever heard a more manly, gruff sound. I liked it. "Kat, this is Sleepy Hollow. I'll make a report for you, but…that's about all I can do. Nothing was stolen that you know of, right?"

What the hell did that have to do with anything? I shook my head. It wasn't like I'd taken a log of my dad's stuff the exact moment I got here.

"We get calls like this all the time. Windows suddenly open, everything's moved a bit, nothing taken," Bones explained, holding his hands on his sides, puffing out his chest a bit. Or maybe that was just his chest, so big and wide and…ugh, so fucking strong. I bet his pectorals were as hard as rocks. "There's little else I can do besides write up the report."

Despite his drop-dead gorgeous appearance, his words caused me to simmer a bit. "Don't tell me you're saying there are ghosts in this town who like to pop in and mess stuff up." *Please, really. Don't tell me. You're too cute to be crazy like the rest of this town.*

"We would never say that officially," Bones said with a shrug. "But things around here aren't like how they are in the big city. You should know that by now. The longer you're here, the stronger you'll feel it."

"I spent every summer here from when I was five years old until I was eighteen. If I haven't felt it by now, I'm not going to. And I'm not staying. I'm doing what I have to, putting the house on the market, and then I'm out."

Bones took a step closer to me, and he was so close I could smell him. Some kind of body spray or hair gel or something—whatever it was, it smelled *good*. Made my insides all tingly and shit. Or maybe it was just his face; his jaw was a lot squarer than I remembered it being.

"You should stick around for a while," he said, his voice sweeping over me like a smooth wave caressing the shore. "It's not a bad place to live. You might like it here." A dimpled smile spread across his face, the blue in his gaze lighting up. "I could make it a habit to swing by, make sure all of your windows are shut."

Was he coming onto me? Was he flirting? We'd been friends before but this…this was new territory. I didn't know how to handle a flirting Bones. A man like him had to have a girlfriend or a wife anyway, right?

So, me being me, I decided to ask in the most ridiculous, roundabout way possible: "I don't think your girlfriend would like the idea of you stopping by so often." Ugh. Talk about being obvious.

His smile widened, dimples deepening. *Oh, those dimples*... "It's a good thing I don't have a girlfriend at the moment then, isn't it?"

I felt my face heat up. "A very good thing." The words were out of my mouth before I could stop them. If I didn't know any better, I'd say *I* was coming on to *him*—which I wasn't because I wasn't going to stick around. This was a one and done kind of thing.

Another step towards me. The man stood less than a foot and a half away from me. If I stared straight ahead, I'd stare right at his chest. "I know you plan on leaving, but why don't I give you my number? That way, in case anything like this happens again—or you want to grab a pizza like old times—you can let me know?" The way he offered, as if it was so easy, so simple.

It kind of was, I realized as I handed him my phone, which was resting in my back pocket. I watched him enter his phone number into my phone, wondering why in the world, out of all the cops in Sleepy Hollow, Bones had to be the one to show up on my doorstep ready to investigate. Eh, not so much investigate as tell me this apparently happened all the time and no one ever freaked out about it.

That was…that was weird, but this whole town was weird.

As he handed my phone back to me, he said, "I might not live two streets over anymore, but I'm still close by. If you ever need anything, or if you need help with the planning for your dad, let me know." Bones headed to the door, pulling it open. I tried not to stare at the way a vein bulged on the top of his hand.

Hell, I couldn't even say why, but I found it attractive. He was definitely not the boy I'd grown up with over the summers.

"I'll write up that report for you. If anything else strange happens around here, let me know." Bones started to walk out, but stopped almost instantly. "Oh, and I'd stay away from Crane, if I were you." He was going to leave again, just like that, with those ominous words lingering in the air between us.

Crane didn't seem like a bad guy, even if it was fishy that the office was torn apart just after he left. Could someone as thin as him scale the side of a house? I wasn't sure. Plus, I didn't get the whole bad guy vibe from him.

I moved to the door, holding onto it as I watched Bones head down the porch steps. "Why?" I asked. "What's so bad about Crane?" For a stupid moment there, I felt like I was tossed into the legend itself, caught between a Crane and a Brunt.

"I don't like to spread gossip, but he's…" Bones stopped, his feet on the concrete pathway that led to the sidewalk. "He's weird. He and your dad were up to some weird things, Kat. I would stay away from all of their research. I'd burn it all." A dour seriousness took over his face, but in the blink of an eye, the seriousness was replaced by a smile and wave.

I watched him go, an uneasy feeling rising in my gut. All this cryptic stuff was giving me a sick stomach. I hated how everyone was so superstitious around here. Honestly, besides all that, this town wouldn't be half bad. Alas, everyone's heads were so far stuck up the old legends and stories that they usually forgot this was the twenty-first century, and believing in ghost stories took a special kind of stupid.

At least that's what I thought, until I made the stupid mistake of crossing the bridge at midnight.

Chapter Three

It was late, and I was in the middle of going through all the stuff in the kitchen, choosing what was worth donating to a second-hand store and what was just trash when my stomach refused to be silenced any longer. There was nothing in the freezer that I would trust, and definitely nothing in the fridge I'd want to touch with anything less than a ten-foot pole, which meant one thing: I had to go out and get food.

I tore off the rubber gloves I'd put on—because my dad sure kept some nasty-ass shit, let me tell you—and got to my feet. Even though it'd been years since I'd been here, I knew the town couldn't have changed that much. With my wallet and my phone in my back pockets, I left, swinging the key to the house around my finger after locking up the front door.

The sky was an eerie pitch-black, and even though it was a cloudless night, I could see no stars when I glanced up. Nothing but the moon, which appeared to be full, or close to it, at the very least.

A full moon. It was a wonder why these townsfolk didn't go batshit crazy even more. Weren't full moons supposed to bring out the crazy in people, or was that an old wives' tale?

I took the sidewalk, taking the long way through town to the small convenience store I knew was next to the town's gas station. It was the only place open late, and if I remembered correctly, its prices were low, too. I was on a budget here. This wasn't exactly an all-expenses paid vacation for me.

The convenience store's parking lot was empty, and I headed straight to the glass door, pushing inside. The clerk behind the counter didn't even look up, his nose remaining down as he read whatever paper was before him. No hello, no asking if he could help me find something. Not even a glance.

I went to the drinks in the back, pulling out a few chilled energy drinks. Next came food, and by food I meant snacks. Going through someone's house, deciding what to keep and what to get rid of—it wasn't a job you did while eating full, nutritious meals. It was something you did while you stuffed your face full of chips and other greasy things and hating yourself all the while.

My dad...I loved him, in a weird way. I didn't love him like a kid normally loved their dad, but still. I didn't think I'd get a call from his lawyer, saying that he'd died and I was needed in Sleepy Hollow as soon as possible to discuss the will and make his final arrangements. I thought...hell. I didn't know what I thought. I guess I just imagined that I had more time, many more years left before I'd have to worry about putting either of my parents in the ground.

That was the thing about death. It always snuck up on you, even when you thought you were ready for it. It constantly crept up on you, inching towards you, running at a full sprint at you when you weren't looking, but you could never tell how far it was. Never tell how close it was.

If I would've known my dad was going to die, would I have kept coming to Sleepy Hollow during my time off school? Would I have visited him on holidays and on his birthday? I...I didn't know. Maybe. Maybe not.

But it didn't matter now, because he was gone.

I grabbed a few bags of chips and pretzels off the racks, moving to the front of the store. As I set my stuff down, the clerk was slow to draw his gaze off the paper he was reading. No, wait. Not a paper. A comic book. All it took was one quick glance from me and I knew what the comic book was about.

The Headless Horseman.

Of fucking course. Because no one in this town could lay low and be normal, not even the kids. The clerk must've been around eighteen or nineteen, his skin pale and covered with acne scars.

"Is this all for you?" he asked, sounding bored and monotone, like he didn't want to be here. I couldn't blame him, because I didn't want to be here either. Who would? Who the hell would willingly want to be here, in Sleepy Hollow?

"Yep," I said, my fingers tapping the edge of the pressboard countertop as he rung me out. I handed over the money to pay for it, and he was unhurried in bagging it. My eyes flicked to the clock behind him on the wall, resting just beneath a bright, fluorescent light.

Eleven forty-nine. Nearly midnight. This was the latest I'd stayed up in a while. My college years were full of studying, not staying out late and partying. I was a boring person, really. I hated most people, and was much more comfortable at home on the couch, a bowl of snacks nearby, a book on my lap, and a TV show blaring in the background than anywhere that required socializing.

Don't get me wrong, it was nice to have friends, to talk to someone other than yourself, but most of the time other people were just mean. Mean, awful, and annoying, so I'd rather just avoid them entirely.

I was in the process of grabbing my bags off the counter and leaving the convenience store when the clerk suddenly looked up from his comic book, his cloudy eyes much too intense suddenly. "Don't cross the bridge—"

Don't cross the fucking bridge. Yeah, I got it. I didn't wait for him to finish before heading out the door.

I moved across the empty parking lot, the night air whispering sweet nothings to me as the breeze blew past me. Everyone was always so adamant against crossing the bridge at midnight. Why? It was just a bridge, nothing special. Nothing out of the ordinary.

Everyone warned me to stay away from the bridge, especially around midnight? Newsflash: a bridge was just a bridge. No ghosts, no spirits, no fucking Headless Horseman. I'd take the quicker route back to the house by jogging over the bridge everyone was so worried about.

I had no idea why I was so aggravated by it all, but I was. Today I had it up to my neck with the Sleepy Hollow shit, so I was going to walk over the bridge just to prove everyone wrong and make myself feel a little better about being so judgmental towards the townies. Some people might call it bitchy, but I preferred judgmental.

The bridge everyone was talking about was a boring, nondescript bridge. It was literally just a bridge built of stone archways and wooden railings. In the olden days it used to be a dirt road that went over it, but now it was meant for cars, though each side of it had two extra feet for a sidewalk area.

My feet stopped me just at the base of the bridge. Behind me, the majority of Sleepy Hollow sat, its shops and its houses all black and closed in for the night. Ahead of me was mainly just darkness, the only thing lighting the way the moon. If I didn't spend my summers here growing up, I might've thought it creepy, but I knew my way around the town better than I wanted to admit.

When I was younger, my dad had a small shack just outside of town. Nothing like the huge, gothic house he had now. He had little money, worked odd jobs to make ends meet. He was constantly going on and on about whatever new thing he was doing experiments on. One time he even set the living room on fire.

Fucking seances. Trying to talk to the dead. It had meant nothing to me when I was younger, but now that I was older there was nothing redeeming about any aspect of my dad, besides that he loved me. His love for me was it. The rest of him? Coocoo for Cocoa Puffs.

I heaved a sigh, telling myself to stop thinking about the past. It was in the past, no changing it now. What was done was done. My dad was dead, and apparently whatever he was working on—something about ghosts—was worth trying to steal. Maybe Bones was right. Maybe I should burn it all, then there'd be nothing for anyone to break in and take.

It would be something to figure out tomorrow, I decided. Tonight, I was going to walk over this damned bridge, go back to the house, eat, and sleep. That's it.

My fingers curled around the plastic handles, and I threw a look over my shoulder. No one was around. It was late, a school night, I think. Not a single car on the road. All in all, it was eerie. Or perhaps I was letting this town's superstitious nature rub off on me.

I headed to the center of the road, figuring, why not walk across the bridge like a badass? Ghosts? What ghosts? There weren't such things as ghosts, and this bridge was just a hunk of premodern construction. What was so special about it being midnight, anyway? What was it about midnight that got everyone's panties in a twist?

I was about to find out.

By the time I walked to the bridge from the convenience store, it had to have been near midnight. My feet drew me towards the bridge, taking my first official step off the road and onto the wooden floorboards that made up the bridge's flat top. Step by step, I kept going, feeling rightly proud of myself, considering all I was doing was walking across a bridge. As if it took some kind of special skill.

It didn't. Anyone and their brother could walk across a bridge, but it took someone from Sleepy Hollow some real guts to do it at midnight.

I was just about to laugh at myself, and at this town for making me feel the faintest trace of unease about walking across a bridge, but the moment I reached the middle of the bridge, the temperature of the air around me changed. Instantly dropped at least fifteen degrees, filling my arms with goosebumps.

Eyebrows furrowing, I glanced down at my arms, noticing the way each and every hair on them stuck straight up, like I'd walked into an electrical field. The hair on the nape of my neck prickled, and I blinked, not having any reasonable explanation for this.

Turning my head up, I took another step forward, but the moment I did, it was like I hit a wall, even though there was nothing in front of me. And then— then the craziest thing happened. The world of midnight turned into day, dark became light, stunning me into silence.

My eyes scanned the area. There was no sun overhead, and when I looked upward, I saw only an off-white haze. The colors of the bridge, of the grass and the water below the bridge—nothing was right. Everything was wrong...beside the fact that it should've been nighttime, I mean.

Extra wrong. Things were extra wrong around here.

The hue of everything was too saturated, yet there was a cloud of haze, almost as if a web-like substance covered my field of vision. As far as I could tell, I was alone. I hesitated, about to try to walk forward again. This time I was not stopped by an invisible barrier. This time I was able to walk without any problems. This time I heard something behind me.

The sound of hooves hitting pavement. The loud exhalation of an angry, agonizingly abrupt breath. The low whinny of a horse that sounded both furious and upset.

I froze, my shoulders straightening. This was not happening.

Somehow, before turning around, I already knew what I'd see. In my heart of hearts, I knew exactly who I'd lay eyes on once I spun towards the horse. As I turned, my breath caught in my throat, the air in my lungs turning toxic as I stared at the black horse with burning red eyes. It stood just off the bridge, not far from where I was, twenty feet, tops, nibbling on its bit, pawing at the pavement over and over, waiting for its rider to give the signal.

And its rider…

Its rider was the stuff of nightmares, or urban legends revolving around Sleepy Hollow, technically. Big, wide, like a fucking linebacker, but all muscle instead of pudgy beefiness, wearing all black, an old and torn uniform…and just as headless as the tales said.

The Headless Horseman.

The Headless fucking Horseman.

"Shit," I muttered, taking a step back. My heart beat wildly in my chest, threatening to burst out and run away as if it had two feet of its own. This was not real. This wasn't happening. This was some sort of hysterical hallucination. Was the water contaminated here? Was it something in the air?

This...this just couldn't be real. I refused to believe it.

Still, even though my mind would not compute, I knew I had to get out of there, especially when I saw his chest heave. How the hell did someone without a head breathe? Not something to wonder about right now. The Headless Horseman extended his left arm, and a shimmery, two-sided ax appeared out of nowhere, its blade red and incorporeal, almost like it struggled to maintain its existence.

I didn't stop to think about whether he was going to attack me. Or throw it at me. Or do whatever it was the Headless Horseman did. In the blink of an eye, I turned around, just as he started to lift the ax.

I was not alone with the Headless Horseman.

Behind me, suddenly and strangely, another figure stood. This one was a woman. Less than two feet from me, her hair was nearly as long as her entire body, floating in the air and defying gravity itself. Her flesh was pale, almost see-through, and her eyes…they were all white. No irises, no pupils. Nothing at all but balls of white. In a swift, flash of movement she lifted her arms and bared her teeth, showing me she didn't have the typical human bite. Nope.

Her teeth were like knives. Dozens of teeny, tiny knives that I bet hurt like a bitch sinking into skin.

The woman, who wore a shredded white dress, appeared to be both out of her time and out of her mind. She let out a scream, and my ears instantly ached in pain. I stumbled back, tripping on one of the floorboards of the bridge, landing on my ass.

The very moment I tripped and fell, I stumbled back into the real world, my vividly real hallucination nowhere to be seen. My vision took a few seconds to come back to me, the world around me black. As I blinked, I felt tears well up, and I hurriedly wiped them away and onto my jeans.

My bag had spilled open, its contents sitting on the wood beside me. The sky was black and full of silence, no haze, no off-white color. No woman before me with long, flowing hair and crazy teeth—I threw a look over my shoulder, just to be sure—and no Headless Horseman and his demonic steed behind me.

I was alone once more. Alone and utterly terrified.

As I hurried to shove all of my things back in the bags, I felt my chest. My heart refused to slow down, and my blood pressure felt like it was through the roof. I wasn't one to make things up, but that felt so real, not imaginary at all.

I hurried back to the house, locking the door, breathing hard, for some reason. I went into the living room, setting the bags on the coffee table, plopping myself on the couch. It was an uncomfortable thing, full of springs and a few stains that were questionable, but my mind was elsewhere.

On what I saw.

On what I felt.

I saw the Headless Horseman. He was real. He had to be. Either that, or I was losing it just like my dad did. I would say it was this place, but I spent months here every year growing up. Bones and I got into some wild shit, playing in the cemeteries and all that. Not once did I ever hallucinate.

Granted, I never walked over the bridge at midnight, but…

Damn it. Listen to me, talking about that bridge like it was some gateway to…what did Crane call it? The otherworld? Screw that. I didn't believe in any of this. What just happened was…I didn't know how to describe it; all I knew was that I wasn't hungry anymore, and my eagerness to go through my dad's stuff was gone.

I needed to sleep this off. I needed…well as much as I hated to admit it, I needed to talk to Crane.

That would be a job for tomorrow, I decided, getting up and heading to the stairs. I went into my old room and got ready for bed. I crawled in the sheets, expecting to smell dust on them, but they smelled clean, as if someone had washed them not too long ago. Like someone had expected me. Creepy.

I flopped onto my side, staring at the wall. The comforter was up to my chin, completely covering my body up to my shoulders and neck. I closed my eyes, wishing I'd wake up in the morning and all of this would be some sick, bizarre dream. No Headless Horseman. No bridge. No Sleepy Hollow.

It was a useless wish, and my dreams—once I actually fell asleep—were spent lost in a haze, off-white field, running from something I couldn't see. Even my dreams in Sleepy Hollow were messed up. As I woke up the next morning, light streaming through the window, I knew one thing.

I had to leave this town as soon as possible.

Chapter Four

I waited until ten the next morning to head to the police station. I knew I had his number, but I didn't feel like calling it. I had no idea where Irving Crane lived, but I figured as a local, Bones would. The problem would be to convince Bones to tell me the address, hence why I thought going to see him in person would be better than texting or calling.

I made sure to look nice, doll myself up a bit. I applied a bit of makeup, mostly eyeliner and mascara, and ran my fingers through my auburn hair to undo the knots. Tight jeans, too. Couldn't forget those. Jeans so skin-tight they could make any man do what you wanted him to.

Sleepy Hollow during the day was livelier than it was at night. There were actual cars on the road, people walking on the sidewalks—and of course, it was like they all had to stop whatever it was they were doing and stare at me, mouths agape. They all knew my dad died, so it wasn't a surprise I was here. They really should've expected me, since I was the only family Dad had left.

I did my best to ignore them as I went into the police station. It was a small building that only had about ten squad cars. There wasn't much crime in Sleepy Hollow, mostly because everyone here knew each other—except for break-ins that apparently ghosts were responsible for.

After what happened to me last night, that explanation was beginning to sound a bit less outlandish, I had to admit.

An older woman sat at the reception desk, her silver hair twisted in a low bun. Her eyes flicked up behind thin-rimmed glasses, and she immediately brightened when she saw me. "You're Phil's girl, Katrina," she said, giving me a warm, wrinkled smile.

"Kat," I corrected her. I refused to be called Katrina ever since I learned who my dad had me named after.

"I'm so sorry to hear about Phil," she went on. "When will the ceremony be?"

"I haven't spoken to his lawyer yet, but as soon as I do, I'll let the town know." My dad, for his strange antics and weird experiments, was loved in the town, I guess. Weird. But then again, practically everyone here believed the legends. I…after last night, I wasn't sure what to believe.

The woman nodded, sympathetic. "What can I do for you today, Kat?"

"I was hoping to talk to one of the officers," I said, glancing behind the reception desk. The desk sat in front of a wall of windows, allowing you to see the station's desks behind it, where the officers that were not out on the streets sat and did their research or their investigating. Whatever it was cops did when they weren't pulling you over for speeding. I didn't see Bones.

"Do you need to file a police report?" the woman asked, trying to be helpful.

I shook my head. "No, I need to talk to one officer specifically. Brom Brunt." Brom Brunt. You can see why he liked to be called Bones. It was better than the name he was given, that's for sure.

Suddenly the look on the old woman's face changed, and the smile she gave me made me think she had the wrong idea about why I wanted to see him. "Ooh, sure, sure. Go on back. I'll make a note that you're here for the log. He should be in the office somewhere, unless he slipped out the back door." The woman let out a girlish giggle as she jotted something down on the piece of paper where visitors were meant to sign in.

I really wanted to tell her that I wasn't here for that reason, but I didn't, figuring it'd be too much to explain anyway. Heading around the reception desk, I moved to the door that led to the offices, turning my head as I gazed at the cluttered space. The other officers stopped what they were doing, all of them looking at me.

I really hated how everyone in this town knew me. It was why I did my best growing up not to learn anything about them. Bones had been the only friend I'd needed, and Bones was who I needed right now, not any of these other people.

Bones walked out of a side room, carrying a Styrofoam cup of steaming coffee. A woman was beside him, wearing the same uniform. She had no coffee in her hands, and she was busy looking up at him and laughing, batting her eyes a bit too hard. My jaw clenched, and I resisted my urge to head over there.

I was *not* jealous; I was...

Okay, maybe a part of me was jealous, mostly because I was sure he'd been flirting with me yesterday. Maybe he wasn't flirting; maybe that was just Bones trying to be nice. I didn't know why the thought of him flirting with a pretty coworker riled me up, but it did. Stupid, really, because he wasn't my boyfriend, and he never would be. This town—I'd have it in my rearview mirror soon enough.

I crossed my arms, waiting for Bones to look away from the woman beside him and notice me. Fortunately for my sanity, it didn't take him too long. His blue eyes drifted to me, and his whole face lit up. He was happy to see me, happier to see me than to talk to that woman, which made me feel almost righteous in my misplaced jealousy.

Bones waved off his coworker, and she tried not to look displeased as she watched him walk to me, meeting me in the maze of office desks. "Kat," he said, stunning me by holding his coffee out to the side to hug me.

Yes. Hug me. Like we didn't see each other yesterday.

Just when I was about to relax and let myself be hugged, maybe even hug him back, Bones released me, grinning a dimpled smile as he took a small sip of his coffee. "What are you doing here?"

"I was hoping I could ask for your help," I said, trying not to focus on the strange feeling inside of me. My nerves about being back in Sleepy Hollow were nothing compared to the swirling emotions trapped inside of me when Bones smiled at me like that. Once you had a huge crush on someone, you never went back, apparently.

"Sure," Bones quickly said, gesturing for me to follow him. He brought me to a desk in the back of the office space, sitting me in the seat across from his. He set his coffee on his desk, which was cluttered with a bunch of papers he immediately sought to stack and move aside. It reminded me of the way he was always embarrassed when I came over and saw his room was messy. He always told me to wait in the hall while he straightened up as fast as any human possibly could.

I let him do it, knowing he wouldn't stop until he was satisfied with how his desk looked, and a small smile tugged at my lips.

"What can I help you with?" Bones asked once his desk was clear. Nothing but wood and a computer now. No mess. No disorder. No more embarrassment for seeing his work station messy. His blonde hair was styled to the side with some light gel, and I had the weirdest thought as I glanced at it.

What would it feel like to run my fingers through that hair?

Ugh. No.

Things were too complicated now that we were adults. We were tame as teenagers and kids, because we grew up together, saw each other's embarrassments constantly. We were friends. But now? We'd spent many years apart. He was now a full-fledged man and I was…I was a woman who was well-aware of his manliness, of his muscles and his dimples and his square jaw.

"I, uh, was hoping you'd be able to tell me where someone lived," I said, speaking slowly. Treading carefully was not a strong suit of mine, but after he'd warned me away from Crane yesterday, I had to. Bones didn't want me near Crane, for whatever reason, but I had to see him.

Bones still smiled at me, and my traitorous stomach heated up like a solar flare beneath that dimpled smile. "Normally we don't give out personal information, but you're coming to me as a friend, right? Not a citizen in need of an officer's help."

I nodded, running my palms over my knees. If I said I wasn't sweaty, I'd be a liar. My skin was a bit clammy. I blamed Bones for it, and the stupid crush I had on him growing up. Now that I was an adult, I knew what the feelings inside of me were: I wanted to jump Bones's bones.

He leaned forward, resting his forearms on the desk. I pretended not to notice the way his sleeves tugged on his muscles, or how large his hands looked. Those hands…I bet they could do a lot. "Who do you need help finding?"

I bit my bottom lip, and Bones's gaze fell to my mouth, lingering there for longer than was polite. I didn't address it though, mostly because I was internally fretting about how to bring Crane into this conversation without making him upset. "Promise you won't get mad?" I asked.

His chest rose and fell with soft laughter. It wasn't the worst sound I'd heard, not by a long shot. "Get mad at you? Kat, I didn't even get mad at you when you stopped coming. I just missed you."

Wow. Way to make me feel guilty about asking for Crane.

"I need to find Irving Crane," I muttered, speaking quietly.

The expression on Bones's face changed instantly, and he leaned back in his chair, eyeing me up in a way that wasn't cold or cruel but curious. He did his best to hide his annoyance as he said, "And why would you need to find him? I told you yesterday to stay away from him."

"And I'm my own person who can make my own decisions, Bones," I told him, not having any of his protective attitude. "Besides, it isn't like I *want* to see him. It's something to do with my dad."

When I brought up my dead dad, Bones's face softened. "I never understood why your dad was working with him. The things they were doing…don't go digging into his research too much, Kat. Bad things tended to happen. You don't know how many times the fire station got a call about fires your dad claimed he didn't start—"

I wasn't here to learn about the fires, or whatever else had happened while my dad was still alive. "I'm here to find Crane. Please, Bones."

His mouth pursed, and he thought about it. I knew an internal war raged in his head. To tell me or not to tell me. It took him a few moments to say, "I'll do you one better. I'll take you to him, but on one condition."

I agreed without hesitation. "Of course. Anything." Well, anything that didn't involve me swearing off of seeing Crane in the future. I hoped Bones understood why I couldn't go and do that.

"I take you to Crane, you talk about whatever you have to talk about, and then tonight I take you someplace I want to take you." His cheeks flushed somewhat. "A date. I'm asking you out on a date, if it wasn't clear before."

There were a few things I could've told him. I could've asked him why taking me out on a date mattered when he knew I was just going to leave town after I dealt with my dad and his house. I could've told him that the last thing I wanted to do was spend a night around the town. Hell, I could've told him no, that I'd give Google a try and see what I came up with when it came to Irving Crane.

All those things I could've said, and this was what came out of my mouth: "Sure."

Sure. I'd heard cooler things come out of a five-year-old's mouth.

The one-word answer was all Bones needed to hear though, for the toothy grin that spread on his face after was unmatchable. "Great," he said, grabbing his coffee as he got up. "You ready to go now? It's a slow day in the office."

Eh, I bet every day around here was a slow day in the office, but I kept my comments to myself as I got to my feet and followed him out of the station. He took me to his squad car, opening up the passenger's side for me, holding the door open. A total gentleman. I honestly couldn't remember if any guy had ever opened a car door for me.

Bones got in the driver's seat, setting his coffee in the holder between us. The squad car was complete with its camera, a caged window between the front and the back seats, and also a huge radio.

As he started driving, pulling us out onto the road the station was on, Bones said, "I take it you didn't listen to me and burn it all." He shot me an easy smile, letting me know he was at least somewhat joking.

Partially joking, but also partially serious.

"No, but I did start to go through the kitchen stuff," I said, gazing out the window, watching as the familiar buildings passed us by. "He had a lot of crap, and I don't think he ever cleaned the house." But then I remembered how my sheets smelled clean, and I shut right up. Things were…peculiar around here.

Bones chuckled, one hand on the wheel and the other leaning against the window. An easygoing posture, one that took me back to our teenage years, when I'd first had the stunning realization that this guy was kinda cute.

Forget the *kinda* part, though.

"Your dad was a strange one," Bones nodded along. "But he was a good guy. Everyone around town loved him."

"The town lunatic," I muttered.

"The lovable town lunatic," Bones corrected me. "And you know everyone around here. They love all that stuff. When there are a lot of tourists in town, sometimes the city council paid your dad to put on a show, talk about his research, the spirits and the Headless Horseman and all that. The tourists loved it."

I drew my gaze away from the window, watching as Bones smiled in memory.

"I remember one time he did it while he was under the weather. I happened to be driving by, just getting off work, and I heard screaming." Bones laughed. "Turned out your dad had the flu, and he threw up all over a pair of tourists who were in the front row. I don't think I've ever been so disgusted, but it was hilarious. Your dad was ready to keep on going, too."

I chuckled softly. That did sound like something my dad would do. Not take his sicknesses seriously. "He never went to the doctors," I whispered. "He used to say no illness was going to take him."

Bones had heard my dad say the same thing many, many times. "But this town would."

We both quieted. This town wasn't what killed him. His obsession, his need to do whatever it was he did—it wasn't what ended his life. I wasn't certain what he died from, but it was something I wanted to talk to his lawyer about, if that blasted Mike would ever call me back.

I…I didn't want to talk about my dad anymore.

"So," I tried to change the subject, "where are you going to be taking me tonight? What should I wear? Keep in mind, I didn't think I'd be going on any dates while I was here, so I didn't pack any fancy clothes."

Sleepy Hollow and fancy didn't belong in the same sentence together, I was aware, and so was Bones. He glanced at what I wore now, and I felt the need to squirm in the seat. "Wear what you're wearing now." Sort of a suggestion, sort of a command.

All I could do was nod.

Bones drove us to the part of town with the huge, old houses. Most of them had been kept up through the years, their big, spacious yards well-manicured and their driveways long and winding. He stopped his squad car on the curb of the street, turning it off before getting out. He met me on the sidewalk, and for a moment, we both glanced at the house an acre or so back.

Giant trees lined the driveway, leading to a white, three-story house. It looked like it was taken straight out of a history book, with columns and archways and even a damn fountain. Way too rich and hoity-toity for me. I didn't even know what you did with a house this big.

"This is it?" I asked, not sure why I bothered. Of course it was. Bones wouldn't stop in front of a random house when I'd specifically asked him about Crane.

"This is it," Bones muttered, thumbs hooking through his belt, where his gun and a bunch of other things sat. Like a toolbelt for cops. His sapphire eyes were heavy as they moved to me. "Do you want me to go up there with you?" The way he offered, one of his feet already pointed toward the driveway to Crane's house, I could tell he hoped I'd say yes. He wanted to supervise our meeting, but I was an adult, and I could handle myself.

Plus, in a house that big, there had to be a frying pan somewhere.

"No," I said. "I'll be fine." Not knowing what I the hell I was doing, I took a step toward him and set a hand on his arm, squeezing gently. Damn, this man had muscles, nice arms, and he looked amazing in his uniform. I never thought I had a weakness for a man in uniform, but that was before seeing Bones as a cop. "Thank you." It was much harder to say those two words than it should've been. I blamed the muscles, and my stupid need to touch him just now.

Though Bones wasn't too thrilled about me heading up to Crane's house alone, he smiled at me, and I was probably a few seconds too slow in dropping my arm. "I'll pick you up at six," he said, "unless you need me to wait here—"

"No," I said. "I can find my way home from here." I knew all of Sleepy Hollow like the back of my hand. I knew how to get home from the rich part of town; I just needed his help to figure out what house belonged to Crane. "I'll see you tonight."

Bones nodded, sluggishly returning to his squad car. His eyes met mine across the metal top, and for a moment, we both just stared at each other. Such a ridiculously handsome man, not a thing about him I'd change. He'd make any woman swoon. Hell, he'd make any woman fall to their knees and spread their legs for him.

Something tugged at my heart when I thought about Bones with any other woman. I couldn't say why, but it felt like a betrayal, almost—which was ridiculous, because Bones wasn't mine. He didn't belong to me.

He was a free man, free to go off and sleep with whoever he liked. He wasn't mine, and he never would be.

Heaving a sigh, I was the first one to turn away from our staring contest, and I gathered my courage as I headed up the long driveway to the intimidatingly tall house.

Irving Crane, here I come.

Chapter Five

The front door had no doorbell. I stared at the walls around the door for far too long before I realized that a metal knocker was fixed to the middle of the door, unpainted, its bronze color dull. It was a lion, the round knocker in its mouth. My hand went for it and used it to knock a few times.

Rich people and their useless shit never ceased to amaze me. This was just...old useless shit. I mean, what if you were upstairs and didn't hear the knocker? How long was a person supposed to knock?

I needn't have worried so much, because in less than a minute, Crane was opening the door, his wallet in his hand. "Oh," he said, studying me behind his glasses. "I thought you were here with cookies." He flipped his wallet shut and slid it in his back pocket.

He thought I was a girl scout? That...made no sense, but somehow it didn't surprise me when it came to Crane. He seemed a bit weird, the perfect match for my dad.

We stared at each other for a long time, neither one of us saying anything. I was quiet because I didn't know what to say, while Crane was…just Crane. He was a strange one, a person I wasn't sure how to handle yet.

When the silence became overbearing, I asked, "Aren't you going to invite me in?"

"Oh, yes," Crane muttered, almost like he temporarily forgot his manners. "Yes, do come in. I can make us some tea." He gave me his back, and I trailed him inside.

I could honestly say this house was the fanciest, most over-the-top rich house I'd ever been in. Granted, it wasn't much of a competition, but still. Everything was expensive, even the paintings on the walls. Most of them, I noticed, were of Sleepy Hollow.

The kitchen was in the far back of the house, looking like it was taken straight out of one of those HGTV episodes. White-painted cabinets, subway tile, a darker grey countertop that was either marble or granite, light fixtures that sparkled. I hated standing in it, mostly because I felt like I was going to dirty it up by touching something.

I slid into one of the barstools on the island, resting a cheek on a hand as I watched Crane fiddle around, making me more tea I wouldn't drink. I had no clue what to make of this guy. Not once in my entire life growing up had I met him, which was why this whole thing was a bit awkward.

After a while, he set a warm cup in front of me, standing near the island as he sipped his own mug. Crane observed me like I was some foreign animal, a creature he'd never seen before, something he didn't even know was real.

"Is there a reason you're staring at me like some kind of science experiment?" I questioned, turning my head towards him. My stare caused him to look away; at least he had the decency to look sorry for ogling me like a newly discovered species.

"Apologies," Crane said. Today his thin shoulders wore a dark blue dress shirt, every single button buttoned, save for the topmost one. I bet that was his letting loose. His long legs wore black pants that probably cost an arm and a leg. He looked like he was ready for a business meeting, some CEO chilling, lounging about in his million-dollar house. "I didn't expect to see you here, not after yesterday."

I scratched the back of my neck, my auburn hair falling over my shoulders. The whole frying pan incident was not something I was proud of, the more I thought about it. "I am sorry about that," I muttered. "I wasn't expecting anyone. My dad never told me he was working with someone."

"That's because you never called him," Crane said, and I shot him a glare, to which he flinched.

"You didn't happen to see anything yesterday as you were leaving, did you?" I asked, remembering the tossed around office. As Crane shook his head, I added, "It's funny, because right after you left, I heard a noise upstairs. Someone was in my dad's office, rifling through this stuff...kind of like what you were doing when I caught you."

Crane adjusted his glasses. He was a tall and lanky fellow, but there was a leanness to him. His brown hair was coiffed to the side in a haircut that was not exactly in style. His face was gaunt, refined in the way I imagined royalty to be. In a way, Crane was royalty—royalty of Sleepy Hollow. He was cute, but so not my type. Way too weird for me. Too much like my dad.

"I suspected as much, but I doubt they found what they were looking for," Crane said. "I couldn't find it either, although I hardly had enough time to search."

I could only blink in confusion. "What are you talking about? You knew someone went through the office?"

"I suspected they would try," Crane clarified, his green eyes meeting mine. "But I would bet they didn't find it."

"Find what?" I watched Crane start to leave the kitchen, and I hopped off the stool and followed him. We headed up the stairs.

"The journal. Your dad's journal."

That's what all of this was about? I harrumphed like a ninety-year-old woman who'd just yelled at kids to get off my lawn. "Why would someone want his journal?"

Crane took me to what had to have been his office, and I was momentarily shocked. The rest of the house was clean, but this wasn't. Papers, everywhere. Maps of the town. Diagrams of…cemeteries? "Your father's journal contained the truth. I wanted to find it purely so no one else could get their hands on it."

Okay, I'd come here mainly to ask him about the bridge and what happened yesterday at the house, but this…this was way more than I signed up for. "What are you talking about? What truth?"

He leaned on his wide desk, glancing at me. Looking at me as if…as if he knew me. Like he cared about me. Like I was no stranger to him. The intense expression on his face made me feel…something, but I wasn't sure what. Maybe because I was growing more weirded out by the second.

"They're real," he said.

He didn't have to explain, because my mind flashed back. On the bridge, the white, milky sky, the horse and its headless rider, the woman with razor-sharp teeth and hair that looked like a spider web.

"Ghosts," I whispered.

"Not ghosts, spirits. A ghost is a remnant of someone who was once alive. What we have in Sleepy Hollow is an abundance of spirits," Crane said, bending down as he started going through his drawers. "Spirits who want to cross the veil and leave the otherworld for good. Spirits who'll do anything to get what they want—and that's to be here, with us, in the world of the living."

"So they're dead?" Fuck. I had no idea why I was even entertaining this. It was madness. It was crazy…wasn't it?

"They are the undead, those who can never die," Crane said, finding whatever it was he was looking for.

Something small, round, metallic. He held it in his hand, fingers curling around it as he took a step closer to me. I was too shocked at all of this to move. "Once they cross the veil and step foot in our world, they are near invincible. We have nothing to fight them, only ancient tricks that are really only as good as the castor."

Spells. The man was talking about spells.

What?

Crane's emerald eyes fell to the floor between us, to the wooden floorboards that I knew were original to the house's design, newly buffed and refinished. "The veil has been growing weaker for the last twenty-four years. Your father's research proved it."

"Twenty-four?" I echoed. "I'm—" I stopped from saying it: I was twenty-four.

"Yes," Crane whispered. "From the day you were born, the veil has been weakening. Your father didn't find this out until a few years ago, which I think is why he didn't fight for you. He didn't want you to come here, not until we figured out how to re-strengthen it. It hurt him to not talk to you, but…"

This was crazy. This was insane. Everything Crane was telling me was impossible.

Wasn't it?

He shook his head, his eyes closing momentarily. "Someone has to know, or at least suspect of what you are."

"What?" It seemed to be about the only word I could say, the only one that would formulate on my tongue. My return to Sleepy Hollow was just a series of whats.

"Kat," he spoke my name gently, "I truly don't think your father died of natural causes. I believe someone or something killed him, knowing it would bring you back." Crane's hand lifted, and he offered me the small metal object he'd dug out of his desk.

I took it, his accusation reeling in my brain. He thought my dad was *murdered*? By a person? Or by a spirit? The craziness of this whole thing expanded with each passing minute, intensifying and exploding into something I didn't think I could handle. My fingers rubbed across the smooth face of the round metal object. No bigger than my palm, it was a small thing, and I knew just by staring at it that it was old.

Hundreds of years old.

A sense of deja vu swept over me, and I felt a strange recognition as I brought it to my face, feeling as if I'd gazed upon it before. Which was nuts, because I hadn't. I had never seen this thing before, and yet I knew just how to open it. Twist the small button on top to unlock the latch holding it closed. It popped open, and I stared down at a yellowed picture.

A picture of me.

Not of me today, but of many, many years ago. She was a stranger, yet she wore my face. Her hair was curled and pinned to her head, a dress clad on her torso; it was all I could see, but it was enough.

Katrina Van Tassel.

I didn't just look slightly like her; I looked *exactly* like her. A mirror image. A doppelganger. She was me, and I was her.

"You are Katrina Van Tassel," Crane's voice broke into my thoughts, and I met his stare, not knowing what to do or what to say. "You are the missing piece to this puzzle." He slowly reached for me, his hand closing around mine, forcing the locket shut. He didn't pull his hand off mine, letting it linger, the smoothness of his hand about the only thing keeping me sane.

"But…" Another one-word response. I could say no more. "How?"

"Fate, magic?" Crane offered. "Sleepy Hollow doesn't follow the rules of nature. Things are different here." His fingers ran across mine, sending tiny jolts of electricity up my arm. My body was responding to his, and I didn't know why. It was all too much. "You belong here, Kat," he whispered, taking the locket from me and returning it to its place in his desk.

I shook my head. Over and over I shook my head, as if denying it would make it untrue, as if telling him *no* would make my mind forget about that picture. Our faces weren't just similar; they were the exact same. I didn't simply look like all the paintings of Katrina in town…because those paints were of me.

"No," I whispered. This was a bad idea. I shouldn't have come here. My dad, murdered? Spirits, real and undead? The veil and the otherworld—not words I wanted in my vocabulary.

No. I was done with this conversation.

I turned on my heel and hurried out, practically falling down the steps as I went toward the front door, wanting to leave this house and never return. Crane was clumsy in following me, calling out for me to stop, but I didn't hear him. I blocked his voice out on purpose, not wanting to hear him say any more.

Reaching the front door, I yanked it open, taking a single step out.

And then, again, the world turned different. The blue sky morphed into one of ash and grey, no ball of sun anywhere. The colors of the world were a little brighter, off just a hair. But that wasn't what stopped me cold.

That honor belonged to the black horse and its rider, who stood at the base of the driveway. The horse pawed at the concrete ground, its hooves echoing in the air, its maroon eyes glaring at me, even from so far away. And the rider...the Headless Horseman stared at me, too. Or he would be, if he had a head with eyes.

He looked like he was about to heave himself off his demonic steed, but I didn't wait to watch. I stumbled back, tripping over my own feet as I went backward into the house, slamming the door closed.

Crane's arms were around me, his hands holding me upright. I blinked over and over, my vision sluggish in returning to me, and I was back in the real world, staring at the closed door with Crane as my support and tears in my eyes. I wiped them away before he could see them—and noticed they weren't normal tears.

They were tears of blood.

"Oh, Lord," Crane's voice fell on my ears, a welcome sound. "You're like him, only worse. Philip could only hear them, he couldn't see them."

He helped me to the nearest seat in a sitting room of sorts, carefully setting me down on the couch, kneeling before me. I met his stare, my heart still beating wildly in my chest from what I saw.

"What did you see?" Crane whispered, lightly touching my hair, tucking the stray tendrils behind an ear. A gesture that was far too intimate, considering we were strangers to each other, but I didn't stop him or push him away.

All I could stare at were my fingertips, which were stained a dark red from wiping away the bloody tears. "I saw him," I said, being as purposefully vague about it as I could. I didn't want to say it out loud. If I said it out loud, it might make it more real.

This…this was all so much more real than I ever thought it could be. It would take a strongly delusional person to claim this was fake and that none of it was real.

"Him?" Crane asked. "Him who?"

I closed my eyes, wishing I could take a time machine back to the day before I'd learned all of this stuff was actually real. My dad wasn't crazy. He was obsessed, but at least the object of his obsession was real. "The Headless Horseman."

"Oh no," he muttered. "You crossed the bridge at midnight, didn't you?"

I nodded. Such a trivial thing, but it was something that was so ingrained in everyone who lived here, even the children. I didn't think it was a real warning.

"He's after you now," Crane added, standing, looking extra tall from where I sat.

"After me?" I echoed, my voice cracking.

"Your father never saw him, but at least he was smart enough to keep away from the bridge—"

I didn't take kindly to Crane calling me stupid. "Yeah? Well I didn't think any of this was real until I crossed that bridge and saw him! How was I supposed to know all of the legends were real? How was I supposed to know I look exactly like Katrina Van Tassel? My dad never told me any of this stuff." My eyes grew watery, and I buried my face in my hands, not wanting to cry in front of Crane. The bloody tears were one thing, but breaking down completely?

I didn't know why I cared about him seeing me cry, but I did.

Crane quieted for a long while, almost as if he'd never seen anyone start to break down before. I felt a warm hand pat my shoulder as he said, "There, there."

There, there? That's what comforting skill he had? I managed to chuckle, turning my head up to the high ceiling as I muttered a low, "Oh, fuck me." Crane looked shocked I resorted to such crassness, so I added, "Bet the old Katrina didn't swear like that."

"The original Katrina was also in a love triangle between Ichabod Crane and Abraham Van Brunt," Crane said, frowning to himself. "She also couldn't see spirits…so maybe we can use this to our advantage. I doubt they'll suspect your father passed his propensity for them down to you." He began to pace the room, and I watched him walk back and forth with watery eyes.

"I'm not staying here," I told him. "I'm leaving after the funeral and I empty the house."

Crane's long legs abruptly stopped, and the look he gave me right then and there made me want to take it back. "You would forsake all of your father's work because you're frightened?"

"From what it sounds like, my dad didn't want me here anyway. Being here, won't it just make the veil crack more?"

"Weaken," Crane corrected me, and I rolled my eyes. "The veil is weakening, not cracking. But you know what a key can do when used correctly, don't you?" He held a finger in the air, an ah-ha moment dawning on him. "The same key can both open a door and lock it. You—" He turned his finger toward me, and I resisted my urge to slap it away. "—are the key. You've always been the key."

"Great," I said, standing. Crane was easily over six foot, and when I stood, I stood staring at his chest. "Find out how to lock it up in the next week, and I'll help. If not, I'm gone." *If I don't die first, that is…*

Crane moved in front of me, and I found it odd how a man could be both clumsy and smooth at the same time. "You can't leave." I was done telling people I wasn't sticking around after I handled arrangements for my dad, and I was about to tell Crane off when he said, "I mean you can't leave this house, not with the Headless Horseman after you. He'll follow you and either drive you mad or kill you."

He wanted me to stay here, in this house, with *him*? I wanted to laugh, but given everything I'd just learned, I couldn't.

"I'm not afraid of the Headless Horseman," I said, a blatant lie neither of us believed.

"If you're not afraid of him, you should at least be afraid of the spirit who killed your father. They'll be after you, too." Crane took off his glasses, pinching the bridge of his nose as he squeezed his eyes shut. When he opened them, his hand dropping to his side, he whispered, "I know I'm not the easiest person to be around, and I know I might come off as a little unstable and strange, but believe me when I say you should not return to that house. You shouldn't leave my house until we figure out how to at least get the Horseman off your back. My house has wards, the best wards money can buy."

Seemed like a load of bullshit. "And my dad's house doesn't?"

"He wouldn't let me do his house. He liked the spirits and interacting with them. Not all of them are bad, but…" Crane trailed off, slowly putting his glasses back on. "It's always the few that ruin it for the many, and the ones that are bad are viciously vile. Beyond deadly."

"I'm not going to stay here," I told him, and I wasn't. Nothing he could say or do would make me change my mind. As scary as it was, I was going to go back to that house and continue going through all of my dad's shit and pray that his lawyer finally returned my call. I turned to leave, but Crane grabbed my hand.

He didn't hold onto it long, but even after he dropped it like a hot potato, I still felt the aftereffects of it. His hands were so smooth, yet they could be firm, too. "I'm sorry. I just don't want to see you get hurt, or worse. If you came back to Sleepy Hollow only to be killed by the Headless Horseman, I—"

"I'll be fine," I said, hoping that by stating it I would start to believe it. "Tell you what. If you happen to find anything…stop by. I'll let you in, no frying pan this time."

"At least let me drive you home." Crane heaved a sigh, and the sound fell over me like honey. The longer I spent around him, the more I was starting to like his odd quirks and his overly eager way of saying everything, which was bad. I shouldn't like him, and I definitely shouldn't still have feelings for Bones.

Fuck it all to hell.

I was just like my namesake, wasn't I? Meant to waffle between two men until one of them claimed me as theirs. Yuck.

Chapter Six

It was near impossible for me to do any more work that day. I paced through the house for a long time before saying screw it all and getting ready for the date. It wasn't like I could call up Bones and tell him I'd changed my mind.

Well, technically I could, but I'd feel really shitty about it. Plus, going out on the town—as much of a town Sleepy Hollow was—would help me get my mind off of everything I learned today. Surely the Headless Horseman would leave me alone, at least for a little while. Give a woman a break, you know?

I was fucking Katrina Van Tassel. I was able to see spirits in the otherworld sometimes. Oh, and who could forget the Headless Horseman was after me because I made the stupid mistake of crossing that bridge at midnight? Totally my own fault, there. And let's throw in the whole my-dad-might've-been-murdered thing, because that was kind of a biggie.

Yeah, so far today had been a doozy, and it wasn't over yet.

I did the best I could do with my hair, considering I didn't bring a curler or any hair spray, and changed into a nicer shirt. I kept on the jeans, sliding a pair of ankle-high boots on under them.

Bones pulled up in front of the house right at six, on time to the minute. I knew because I was sitting in the living room, wondering just how my life had gotten to this crazy point. It was honest-to-god crazy how fast my life had been turned upside-down. Everything I thought I knew, everything I always shook my head at as I was growing up…it was all real.

Did everyone else know about it all? Did Bones? Bones thought I should stay away from Crane…was it because he didn't want me involved in any of that, or because Bones was like I was a few days ago, ignorant of how Sleepy Hollow truly was?

It didn't matter. I wasn't going to bring up any of that stuff while on the date. I was going to try to enjoy myself, to get those things out of my head and have a good time. I needed a good time, otherwise I might just go as nutzoid as my dad.

I met Bones near his car. His real car, not his squad car. It was red and sporty, and I instantly liked it. He was leaning on the hood, his thumbs jammed into his pockets as he watched me approach, grinning boyishly. "I'd say you look good, but you always look good, Kat," he said, flashing me his straight, pearly white teeth.

I always looked good? Screw that. He looked good. He wore a plaid shirt, the sleeves rolled up to his elbows in the kind of way that made me weak at the knees. Something about rolled-up sleeves drove me crazy. Like he was ready to throw down if needed, get wild and rough and dirty and…

Not a train of thought I should be having while staring at him like I'd never seen a finer man.

Had I, though? Out of pure curiosity, had I ever seen a finer man? Didn't think so.

"You don't look half bad yourself," I muttered, hating instantly how I was trying to play it cool. There was no cool with me. It was just different levels of awkwardness, apparently.

Once we were in the car, Bones brought us to one of the nicer restaurants in town. You know, the kind where the waiters wear black vests and white shirts? The kind where they charge you five bucks for a glass of water? Yeah, that kind. Needless to say, I did my best to steer clear of this particular restaurant growing up. It wasn't a place for kids. It was made for adults to have serious conversations over expensive dinners and late lunches.

Not real lunches, though. Lunch was a poor man's meal, I guess.

The waiter sat us outside, and once he took our order, he was off. I stared at Bones over the white tablecloth, watching as he picked at the bottom of his shirt. He'd left the top few buttons undone, allowing me to see the edges of his sculpted chest. It wasn't too hard to imagine myself running a hand down it, breaking open a few more buttons along the way. Bones was as smoking as a man could get. So hot he was practically on fire.

"You know," I broke the table's silence after we got our drinks, "for someone who wanted to take me on a date, you're awfully quiet." I sipped my drink—just water. I didn't want to get any alcohol because if I'd learned anything after today, I had to be alert and aware of my surroundings at all times. Never knew when the Headless Horseman might make an appearance, not to mention whatever other spirits were in this town, having fully crossed the veil.

I asked Crane about it when he drove me home…the answer wasn't a pretty one.

"I'm sorry," Bones spoke, blue eyes meeting mine. He'd shaved after work, not a trace of stubble on his tan jaw. His blonde hair, cut shorter on the sides, was spiked up a bit, and it made me wonder just how much this whole date meant to him. I'd thought it was merely a ploy to spend more time with me, but...

Was this a real date? Did Bones really want to date me?

The thought made me happy—which was odd. I mean, we grew up together. I'd seen him through his dorky phase and his gangly phase. He saw me through braces, my acne-riddled year of ninth grade, and when I ate so much candy from one of the town festivals that I threw up all over his shoes.

We weren't the same kids we were back then. Time had changed both of us, though I felt like it had its hand on him a little more. There was almost no trace of the boy he was; everything about him was full-on, red-blooded American man.

But, even so, the notion also made me feel conflicted, because even though I was attracted to him—because hell, look at him. Who wouldn't be attracted to him?—this couldn't last, unless he was willing to leave Sleepy Hollow to continue to see me. I wasn't going to live here, and I knew that once you were a townie, you were always a townie. You never left Sleepy Hollow.

"Why are you sorry?" I asked.

"I'm nervous," he said, laughing at himself. "It's stupid. I've known you forever. I shouldn't be nervous." He was mainly talking to himself now, trying to muster up his courage to be on this date with me.

I made Bones nervous?

"You're not the only one," I said, shrugging. "It's been a long time, Bones. Being nervous just means you care, right?" He grinned, agreeing with me by nodding. "So, tell me what you've been up to these years without me."

Turned out, Bones had been busy. He went to the police academy, graduated and got a position in Sleepy Hollow. He'd bought his parents house and fixed it up while his parents downsized and got a smaller place. It didn't sound like he had any time to himself.

We had our food before us. I ordered some pasta alfredo while Bones got some kind of chicken parmesan. Our plates looked delicious, but still not worth whatever they cost. I twirled my fork in the noodles, lifting it to my mouth as I said, "How's the dating life around here?" I'd mainly meant it as a joke, but...well. Also seriously.

He shook his head. "Oh, you know, I haven't had much time to date. I'm pretty focused on my work and the house." Bones stuck his fork in a piece of chicken, his azure stare lingering on me, instilling a warm feeling deep within me. "I haven't dated much. Have you?"

Under the table, I had to cross my legs to try to ignore the hungry longing in my core. How long had it been since I'd had sex? I couldn't even remember. "Not a lot, no. There were a few, but…" I trailed off. "None of them lasted long. It's like—"

"You couldn't get into them," Bones finished, and my mouth dropped. Those were nearly the exact words I'd been about to say. What the hell?

"How did you—"

"Because I felt the same," he said, eyeing me up as if he couldn't believe the coincidence either.

I found myself laughing, really wishing I hadn't sworn off alcohol for the night. Now would be a nice time to pop a bottle and take a few, extra-long swigs of whatever it was, even if it burned my throat on its way down.

"I thought about you a lot, Kat."

Those words made me freeze. He thought about me a lot. I…I used to think about him a lot, especially the first two years of college, right after I'd stopped visiting my dad and Sleepy Hollow when I'd turned eighteen, but eventually thoughts of him stopped coming. Or at least they stopped being so frequent. Anytime I caught myself thinking about him, I pushed him aside, because then I'd start to think about my dad and this town, and I didn't want to lose myself in Sleepy Hollow like Dad did.

Once I regained myself, I managed to ask, "Why?"

He looked at me then. Really, truly looked at me. Bones looked at me so hard I could feel his stare in my soul. He could see me, all of me, and he refused to look away. I wasn't just the daughter of the town weirdo; I wasn't the namesake (and apparent reincarnation) of Katrina Van Tassel. I was just me, and the way he looked at me right now made me feel like I was enough.

"I liked you," he said.

"You did?"

Bones nodded. "I thought you knew."

I refused to believe it. "I—I liked you, too." I hurriedly spoke the words, fearing that if I took my time in saying them, I'd think better of it. If he liked me and I liked him...fuck. We missed out on a lot of summers where we could've made out and done other stuff. Were we both really so blind?

Now it was Bones's turn to say, "You did? I didn't...wow. We are both huge idiots, aren't we?" He grinned, his dimples making an appearance, and for a moment, we both laughed at our stupid younger selves.

If only we could get that time back, I knew I'd do things differently. Alas, that wasn't how life worked, so here we were today, laughing about it like it didn't matter. The thing was...it did matter. It mattered more than I could've imagined.

His blue stare crinkled a bit, and his eyes dropped to my chin. "I wish I would've known. Would've given me the confidence to tell you that I liked you."

"And if you would have told me," I chimed in, weaving my fingers together as I leaned on the table, "I would've had more confidence to tell you." It worked both ways, dork. A sexy, manly, infuriatingly hot man, but still a dork deep down.

He could've been *my* dork, if things had been different.

"True," Bones finally relented, his smile deepening into something more, something...that made my stomach harden. Suddenly reaching over this table, grabbing him by the collar and pulling his mouth to mine didn't seem too crazy. If anything, I wanted to do it.

Him, in other words. I wanted to do *him*. I wanted to bend over and let him take me like an animal, or ride him until he exploded. Either way, I didn't care. All I knew was that there was an aching, burning need between my legs, and sitting here and eating this fancy meal wasn't going to cut it.

Not for long, at least.

The need to get ahold of his dick didn't even go away when he brought up Crane, the single subject I wanted to stay away from at all costs—which meant one thing. I craved this man like my body craved chocolate when I was on my period. "How did your conversation with Crane go today?" As he hedged, he held my stare, trying to see if...if what? If I felt something for Crane?

Oh, the man was tall and lean, but weird, and he reminded me entirely too much of my dad. Me and Crane would never happen. Me and Bones, on the other hand...that was much more realistic.

I wrinkled my nose. "Do you really want to talk about Crane?"

His wide shoulders rose and fell with a chuckle. "Maybe not. Let's talk about you. Tell me what you've gotten yourself into while you were away." *Away*, as if I was always meant to come back. Back to Sleepy Hollow and back to him.

So I talked about myself for a while, as boring as it was. I had no interesting stories. Mine was: graduate high school, go to college, graduate there, and, here's the big surprise, get a shitty-paying job in the retail field because my degree was near useless. Useless degrees weren't something colleges told you about, and most parents nowadays, including my mom, bless her, were clueless as to which fields would be hiring in four years.

Ah, well. Not only hiring but paying well.

"You could move back here," Bones said. "You have a house. You could get a job here." He was about finished with his meal now, and he pushed the plate aside. A light breeze blew past us, tickling my nose as I stared at him.

Move back here? Live here, where things were trying to kill me? Where something might've killed my dad? If Bones knew the truth, surely he wouldn't suggest something like that to me. Surely he'd understand why I had to leave Sleepy Hollow and never come back.

"This town," I said, a chill sweeping over me, causing me to shiver, "is not where I belong."

"Then where do you belong?"

My mouth opened, and I was ready with a snarky comment along the lines of *anywhere but here*, but when I saw his earnest expression, I stopped. He'd only take something like that as an insult, so I couldn't say it. Instead I found myself whispering, "I don't know."

And it was the truth. I didn't know where I belonged, but I knew it wasn't here. Not with the spirits and all the other weird stuff that was apparently real. I couldn't belong here. I'd go crazy just like my dad if I stayed here, assuming it was safe.

The look Bones gave me then made me feel bad, and I ignored it as I finished eating. Bones paid for the meal once the waiter brought the check, and I walked with him to his car. I had no idea if this was it—if this was our date—but ever since admitting I didn't know where I belonged, I hadn't felt right.

I felt bad, actually. I could tell I hurt him by saying I didn't belong in Sleepy Hollow, but I didn't know why. It wasn't like I told him I didn't belong with *him*. If I'd done that, it'd be a different story.

We got in his car, and once again, he held the door open for me. He had a habit of doing that; if he didn't knock it off, a woman might start to get used to such treatment. A woman might start to miss such things when she left Sleepy Hollow.

Dusk had taken over the landscape, but it wasn't dark quite yet. Bones glanced at me, his blue eyes twinkling. "There's one other place I wanted to take you, if you're still up for it." His tone was unsure, and I hated that I'd made him rethink this whole thing.

I reached for him, seeking to comfort him by placing my hand on his arm. "I'm up for anything," I said, and I meant it. I didn't want tonight to end, mostly because it meant I had to face facts that this—Bones and I—could never be.

Bones smiled, and he took us…to the cemetery. One of them, anyway. The oldest one in town. The one that was nestled in between pine groves, the one with a small creek running through it. It was such an old cemetery that no one had been buried in it for ages. Growing up, all the funerals that I'd seen during my summers always led to one of the other cemeteries.

This one…had a lot of history. Old headstones, their limestone faces washed off due to the acidity of the rain. Most of them you couldn't even read anymore, the lettering so dull and washed away.

This also happened to be the cemetery Bones and I spent a lot of time in as kids, playing hide and seek and tag and all that. Generally being kids, bored during the summer. He always ditched his school friends to hang out with me. I guess that should've been my clue that he liked me a bit more than a friend.

We parked in the pebbled lot just outside the cemetery's gate, and Bones was slow to unbuckle his seatbelt. I sat there for a moment, wondering if it was even smart to go walking through a cemetery when the Headless Horseman was after me.

Fuck. The more I thought about it, the crazier I thought I was. I hadn't seen or felt anything since this morning, at Crane's house. Not a single thing. Maybe I'd made it all up. Maybe this place was causing my imagination to overexert itself…or maybe the Headless Horseman was just biding his time.

There was only one way to find out.

I got out of the car, breathing in the musky air as deeply as my lungs could handle. All around me, nothing but nature. The town had left the cemetery and its surrounding woods alone, mostly. There was no one else here but us.

Bones walked beside me, rubbing the back of his neck as he glanced at me. "I thought we could take a little walk, kind of like how we used to." Dropping his arm, he tentatively found my hand, his rough, calloused fingers intertwining with mine ever so slowly, wordlessly asking me if it was okay to hold my hand.

It was, but just for tonight.

He took me through the gate; it was an old stone archway with a metal iron gate that no one ever locked these days. Why bother? Nature had already taken everything from the gravestones, all of the names and the dates, and the families of today wouldn't be able to find the headstones of their ancestors. We started walking through the rows of headstones, the giant trees towering around the area. It was a peaceful night, a bit eerie to be walking in a cemetery at night, but still peaceful.

At least it was until Bones said something I wasn't expecting: "Kat, I have to be honest. I still like you. I don't think I ever stopped." The hand holding onto mine squeezed, and our legs slowed.

I gazed up at him, wanting to say the same—for at least a part of it was true. How else could I explain the easy way I felt around him? How else could I explain why I felt so drawn to him? It was like I never stopped crushing on him, even though I hadn't seen him in years. But I couldn't, because I got so lost in his eyes, their dark blue hue, and the way his lips were parted slightly.

Fate.

Was it fate? Did I believe in fate? I wasn't sure. At this point, I didn't know what I believed in anymore. This town had turned what I thought I knew inside-out and upside-down, twisted it up a bit, and then threw it all in a blender, handing it back to me as some unrecognizable substance. I didn't know if I believed in fate, but in this instance, if I did, I'd say I believed my dad was always meant to die so young.

How could I ever agree to that?

As I stared up into his eyes, their blue hue shrouded in the darkness of the night, with the cool breeze nipping at my back, I was unable to say anything in reply, but it didn't matter—because even if I had something to say, even if I begrudgingly agreed with him and told him I still had feelings for him, I wouldn't have been able to say them.

Why?

Oh, no big reason.

Just that his lips were suddenly on mine, stifling any words I would try to say.

Brom Brunt was kissing me, and the worst thing about it was…

I was loving it.

Chapter Seven

Bones had yanked me to him, the hand holding mine releasing me only to snake its way around my lower back, keeping my chest pressed against his. His other hand went for my neck, tilting my chin up. His eyes were half-lidded, semi-closed, and the moment his mouth met mine, I closed mine, too.

Kissing Bones was not like kissing anyone else. I'd had boyfriends before who I'd done everything and more with, but when our lips melded together, when our tongues collided in a hungry, wanton display of pure passion, it blew every other kiss out of the water. No other man was in my head when he ran his tongue over my lower lip, nipping it slightly. I forgot about everything else in my past as he walked us backward, our mouths never unlocking, pushing me up against the nearest tree trunk.

Caught between a hard, muscled body and a rough, unforgiving tree. It wasn't the worst place to be. In fact,

I rather liked it, because I liked him. God, I liked Bones so much, so much more than I knew I should.

Our bodies rubbed against each other, molten desire flooding my core as I heard him moan into the kiss when I tangled my fingers in the mop of blonde hair on the top of his head. The world could fade away, cease to exist completely, and I wouldn't care. Not right now. Right now there was only Bones and me, nothing else. No one else.

Years of pent-up longing and passion went into our embrace. I wanted to break away to breathe, to catch my breath, but I was afraid that if I tore my mouth off his, the magic would disappear. The eternal fires of passion would simmer, leaving me to stare at him and wonder whether or not this was all some huge mistake.

Was it? Would I regret this later? I didn't know, and I didn't care. I just didn't care. The only thing I wanted was Bones, and I had him utterly and completely.

His teeth grazed my lip, teasing me as he trailed kisses along my jawline, burying his face in my neck, kissing the tender, sensitive skin just below my ear. I let out a low moan, arching my back against the tree, grinding my hips against his harder. A low rumble came from Bones's chest, and I reveled in the sound. A growing hardness pressed against my midsection, and it wasn't a belt buckle. It was something I never paid much attention to while growing up, because I'd thought they were gross.

His dick. His cock. Whatever you wanted to call it. It felt hard and, from what I could feel, more than average in size. Realizing what he was packing under the waist, I practically mewled like a cat in heat.

I guess I sort of was in heat right now, because the only thing on my mind was Bones, and shedding all of these clothes.

Was it weird to have sex in a cemetery? It wasn't like anyone would stroll up and interrupt us. Was it disrespectful? I wasn't sure, because this cemetery was hundreds of years old, all of the headstones unreadable. It wasn't like there were any recently-dead buried here.

Hmm. Maybe I was just making excuses. Maybe I just wanted to fuck. Maybe I just wanted to find out how good Bones was with his thick, hard dick.

"I've wanted you for so long," Bones murmured against my neck, licking and nipping, sending waves of chilling pleasure down my spine. I held onto him, grinding against his hips, my eyes closed, lost in the sensation of our bodies pressed together. "So long, Kat."

One of his hands moved, starting to travel down my front, undoing the buttons on my jeans. Then the zipper. But he didn't pull anything down; he slipped his hand under them, running his fingers along me in the most earth-shattering way possible.

I let out a fluttery sigh, throwing my head back against the tree. Bones was good with his hands, apparently. He knew just what area to focus on, what to circle, how to slide his fingers back to my entrance and gather some of the slick wetness there, use it to make it feel better. His mouth showered my throat with hungry kisses, and I let him touch me until I felt like I was going to explode.

Either he was ridiculously good, or I was starved for sexual attention. Maybe a bit of both. It didn't take me long to start rocking my hips along his hand, soft sighs escaping me. The budding pleasure in my core took hold of me, and I felt my muscles tensing up. A louder cry came from me as the orgasm shook me, gripping me so hard I wanted to collapse and fall over, but Bones had me, held me up.

And his fingers weren't done yet.

He slipped one inside of me, and with his mouth near my ear, he whispered huskily, "You're so wet."

Yeah, that didn't surprise me at all, considering what was happening and how skilled Bones was. I mean, holy hell. You'd think I'd never been touched down there before with the way my body was reacting. Like it was ravenous. Like it had never known what a real man was, what a true man could do, until tonight.

His finger began to pump in and out of me, and I turned my head to the side, needing to breathe in air that wasn't hot and heavy. My skin felt warm, too warm, like I was going to implode in a sweaty mess. I closed my eyes, sighing as the breeze blew by.

But then…everything stopped. Bones stopped touching me, stopping pushing against me, stopping showering my neck with attention. Everything just stopped, and I was left with an aching core and a hungry heart.

My eyes were slow to open, my heartbeat running a marathon in my chest. I was going to ask Bones just what the hell he thought he was doing, stopping so soon, while we were in the middle of things—because lady blue balls was *so* a thing—but when I opened my eyes, I suddenly understood.

I wasn't in the real world anymore.

Just like before, on the bridge and as I was leaving Crane's house, I was somewhere else. The otherworld?

A place of eternal light, yet no sun in the sky. A place whose sky was nothing but white and hazy, a milky, thick substance. A place where the colors of the grass and trees were off, too saturated and too bright. My vision was cloudy, but that didn't stop me from seeing him.

The Headless Horseman sat on his red-eyed steed over a hundred feet away, deeper in the cemetery. Though my vision wasn't exactly twenty-twenty right now, I was able to see that the names on the stones were miraculously there, as if etched into the limestone only yesterday.

I breathed hard, my body still worked up from what I'd been doing with Bones. What was my body doing right now? Was I slumped over, suddenly passed out with Bones's finger inside of me?

"No," I muttered, my voice sounding like I was caught in the middle of sex. Airy, feminine—you know the kind. I squeezed my eyes shut, willing myself back to the real world, to the world of night, to the world where Bones would be, waiting for me.

When I opened my eyes, I saw that I still remained in this strange place. My hands went to grip the tree behind me as I watched, mouth agape, the Headless

Horseman heave himself off his horse. His dark frame started to head toward me.

Head. Ha-ha. Punny.

But now wasn't the time for puns. Now was the time for oh-shit's and why-me's.

The Headless Horseman wore all black, an old, battered uniform from a time long ago. Knee-high boots, a leather strap across his chest beneath his overcoat, whose bottoms were singed as if it'd been burned. His hands wore leather gloves, not a single ounce of his skin showing. Where his head would be, where his neck would be, it was just…nothing. Like an empty hole, like someone had filed away at his neck until nothing remained.

I wanted to repeat to myself that this wasn't real, but the longer I spent here, the more I believed it was. This was the most time I'd been caught here; usually by now I somehow managed to stumble back into the real world. Every second that ticked by felt like hours. I'd like to say the dread inching up my spine made me feel less hot and bothered, but…well.

I was going to die horny, wasn't I? A terrible way to go.

His footsteps were heavy, loud as they crunched on the grass. The Headless Horseman stood less than two feet before me, and I was still attached to the tree as if it would save me. My cheeks flushed; I didn't want to look at him, but what else was I going to do? I think I'd rather see my death coming.

Slowly, I turned my eyes back to the legendary headless man. Holy fucking hell, he was large. A giant, even without his head. With his head, he had to be at least six and a half feet tall, and unlike most tall people, he wasn't lanky. He was muscled, huge and intimidating in a way most guys just weren't, no matter how badly they tried to be.

I stared at his chest, wide and strong, watching as it rose and fell—like he was breathing. I was too freaked out about dying in the near future to wonder how a man without a head could breathe. Or walk, for that matter.

The Headless Horseman was…a man, a spirit in his own league. I'd never seen anything like him before, never imagined something like him existed. Was it wrong to be attracted to a body with no head?

My stupid horny body. I wanted to smack it, but considering I was about to die, I figured I'd let him do the smacking. Or the cleaving. Or the…whatever he was going to do to kill me.

"I'm sorry I went on the bridge," I whispered, biting back anything else I might've said when a non-corporeal, double-sided ax appeared in his hand. The ax was half as big as I was, yet he held onto it without a problem. The metal between the two blades ended in a point, and he lifted it against my chin. I rose my chin, keeping it above the point, not knowing what would happen to me if he touched me with it.

Would it hurt? Would it burn? Would I become something like him, aimlessly wandering this place? I didn't want to die tonight. I still had so much of my life to live...

The Headless Horseman lowered the ax, but before I could exhale, he grabbed me by the face with his other hand, his leather glove squeezing on my cheeks, around my chin, forcing me to look up. If he had a head, I'd be staring squarely at it, but he didn't, so I only gazed up, flinching, at empty air.

He held me like that for a while, and since he had no head, I had no idea what he was doing. Could he see me? Was he studying me? Did he recognize me as Katrina Van Tassel? Questions like that would be so much easier to answer with facial cues.

"I don't want to die," I whispered, gasping as his gloved fingers dug harder into my skin. Though he had no head, I could've sworn I saw his chest sway a bit, as if he was cocking his non-existent head at me.

Just when I was about to freak out even more, the Headless Horseman released me, the same gloved hand moving to the side, all of his fingers but one curling inward. He was *pointing*.

I didn't know if I should turn my head away from him, for what if it was all a trick and he swung his ax the moment I looked away? But a nagging feeling in my gut told me to look, so I did. My eyes flicked to the side, following his pointed finger.

We weren't alone. On the edge of the cemetery, where the gravestones stopped and met the woods, another spirit stood. The same one I'd nearly run into on the bridge. The woman wearing a dress, cut up into shreds. The one with hair nearly as long as her body, tendrils that floated wherever they pleased, ignoring the laws of physics. The one with tiny knives for teeth and eyes so white and milky you couldn't stare into them for long.

Why was she here? Was she following me, like the Headless Horseman?

"I don't..." I didn't know what the Headless Horseman was trying to say. Choose my death? Pick between the creepy woman and his ax? Neither seemed like a fun choice. I mean, if I had a say in it, I'd choose life. I was twenty-four years old. I still had a few good years left, I think.

Again, his gloved hand gripped my face, forcing me to look back at him. Or, rather, his headless form. He lifted the ax in his other hand a few inches, calling my attention to it. The Headless Horseman was sluggish in releasing my face, the leather on his hand crinkling as he...pointed to himself?

What was he trying to say? See, another reason having a head would make this whole thing so much easier.

The milky white sky began to fade into a starry black night, and as I was thrown back into the real world, the last thing I saw was the Horseman trying to grab me. But it was too late; I was back in my own body and...I couldn't see anything.

I was on the ground, Bones shaking me, holding me to him. "Kat, are you in there?"

My entire world was black. I reached a shaking hand out, touching his warm chest. "Bones," I muttered. "I can't..." It wasn't the first time this had happened, but it was the first time it didn't go away after a few seconds.

I kept blinking, and slowly but surely my vision returned to me. It took at least a minute, I'd say. Wet tears rolled out of my eyes; I couldn't stop them from falling. They were my body's reaction to being trapped in the otherworld for so long. So terribly, terribly long.

When my vision returned, I found Bones staring at me, his blonde eyebrows together. "Your eyes," he murmured. "They were all white." He reached for me, wiping away my tears, and I saw that they weren't normal tears. Not salty, clear water. They were tears of blood.

I sat up by myself, furiously swiping at my eyes, not wanting Bones to see me like this. Like…whatever this was, whatever was happening to me. I was losing it. Sleepy Hollow was not good for me.

"I should take you to the hospital," Bones added, helping me stand. He still had a bit of an erection, but the hot and heavy moment had long passed, and I was too busy in the otherworld dealing with the Headless Horseman to watch as it waved goodbye. "You seized, or something—"

"No," I said, firm. As firm as I could be, considering everything that just happened. It wasn't every day when you came face to face with the Headless Horseman's ax and lived to tell the tale. I then said something, the one thing Bones didn't want to hear: "Take me to Crane's."

"Crane?" Bones was instantly upset; he didn't bother to hide the fury on his face. "What the hell does that freak have to do with this?"

I set a hand on his shoulder, squeezing it gently. I probably looked a horrible sight, so batting my eyelashes at him wouldn't work. "Please," I whispered. "Just take me to Crane."

His mouth flattened into a thin line, and he said nothing else as he helped me back to the car. We drove to Crane's house in silence, and I could tell he hated this. Not taking me to the hospital was bad enough, but taking me to Crane's instead? It was his worst nightmare, especially after what we were doing at the cemetery.

When we arrived at Crane's, I struggled to get out of the car, still feeling weak. At least I wasn't blind, like I'd been earlier, or crying bloody tears. I didn't know why any of this was happening. My dad could hear the spirits, but I could cross the veil and see them? How did that work?

Bones made his way around the car, wrapping an arm around me, helping me up, being my rock as we walked to the front door. At least he'd pulled up the driveway this time.

"I can make it from here," I said, not wanting to further upset him. We were having a nice, lust-filled time, full of kissing and orgasms, and then the fucking Headless Horseman had to show up and ruin it all. Not to mention that crazy spirit woman…

"I'm coming in with you," Bones stated, and that was that. He used the metal knocker to knock on the door, a lot louder than I would've been. The thumping echoed into the night, and I felt a chill sweep over me, too strong to be denied.

Well, great. If Bones heard everything I was about to tell Crane, he'd think I was just as nuts as Crane. I wasn't…was I?

Fuck. Maybe I was. Maybe I was just as batshit crazy as the worst of them.

Chapter Eight

It took Crane an unreasonably long time to come to the door, and that was because he was sleeping, I realized as I studied him in his robe and slippers. Yes, the man wore a robe and slippers like…hell. I didn't even know anyone who wore those things these days. Plus, my head kind of hurt. Sarcastic quips were not going to come easily to me right now.

I pushed inside, right past Crane before he could even register who was at the door. The moment I walked in, my feet stumbled, and both Crane and Bones grabbed me. One on each side. They both tossed an annoyed look at each other as they helped me to the couch in the sitting room.

Crane blinked behind his glasses, glancing between me and Bones. "What…what happened?" He sat beside me, which totally infuriated Bones, who stood scowling, crossing his arms, his muscles bulging. "Blood." Crane was staring at my eyes.

Crap. I thought I'd gotten it all up, but apparently not.

"We were in the old cemetery," Bones answered for me. "And she just passed out."

Crane shot a knowing look at Bones, oddly posturing for a man wearing slippers and a robe. "And what were you two doing in the cemetery?"

"That's none of your business," Bones muttered, blue eyes glaring. If he could've, I think he would've thrown it down with Crane right here and now. Which was ridiculous. All of this alpha male shit was stupid. It wasn't what I came here for.

I wasn't the original Katrina Van Tassel. I wasn't caught in a love triangle.

It was my turn to speak, and I said, "I saw him again." I didn't know why, but saying the words *Headless Horseman* out loud in front of Bones scared me. I didn't want him to think I was just as crazy as my dad and Crane—both of whom turned out to be not so crazy after all.

Bones asked "Saw who?" the same moment Crane's eyes fell to my lap and said "Ah, I see. He is definitely after you, then."

"Who?" Bones questioned, glancing between us. "Who are you two talking about? If someone's after Kat—"

"Brom," Crane spoke dryly. "I fear you wouldn't believe us if we told you." The look Bones gave him right then was all he needed to be forced to add, "Exactly. Now, thank you for bringing Kat to me, but you are no longer needed here."

"You've got to be kidding," Bones said, this time to me. "This is a ghost thing? I told you to stay away from Crane, to burn your dad's stuff. Don't tell me Crane has you thinking—"

I hated the way he spoke to me, like I was a child, too stupid to know that what I was doing was wrong. Here's the thing, though—it wasn't wrong. I wasn't wrong. The person here who didn't know the whole truth of it was Bones, not me, not Crane. "Talking to Crane hasn't affected my thinking at all. You have no idea what I saw, Bones. What I saw was real—and I saw the Headless fucking Horseman." It was impossible for me to not throw a swearword in there. Those things came so easily to me.

"I should've taken you to the hospital." Bones shook his head, looking a strange mixture of sad and angry. Angry with Crane, disappointed in me. He threw his hands up when I started telling him that the hospital couldn't have helped me, interrupting me to say, "I—I need to go. If you change your mind and want a ride to the hospital, call me." He said nothing else as he stormed out, slamming the front door of the house.

I didn't like how upset he was, didn't appreciate the so-called righteous fury Bones had. I mean, yes, I would've thought the same thing a week ago, but now? Now I knew things really were different here.

"Why did he get so mad?" I whispered once the house had quieted, once it was just Crane and I. "He was the one who told me things happened in Sleepy Hollow…" When he came to my house after the break-in, he'd acted as if nothing was wrong.

"Believing in the unexplained is a lot different than believing in spirits." Crane adjusted his glasses, his left knee touching my right. "Most people here are superstitious, but if you put them at gunpoint and ask them if they would give their life to say the Headless Horseman is real, it's a different story."

I understood what he was saying, where he was coming from. I hated that I'd made Bones upset, but I couldn't change what happened, what I saw.

"So, tell me what happened," Crane said. "Leave nothing out."

I told him. I told him about the Headless Horseman, how he'd grabbed me, forced me to look at him. I told him about how he pointed to the other woman at the forest's edge, and then how he'd pointed to himself. My nerves were still fried, and when I thought back to it, I could hardly breathe.

"It almost sounds like he was warning you," Crane said. "This woman, the other spirit, can you describe her more for me?"

I explained the white hair, how it defied gravity, looked almost like a spider web, and all the other aspects about her that I knew. "It wasn't the first time I saw her," I spoke softly. "When I crossed the bridge, she was there, too."

Crane's back straightened. "You didn't tell me this before."

"I didn't think it was important."

"The bridge is the Headless Horseman's territory. For her to be there…it only means one thing." Crane looked pale, or maybe it was just because he wore a white robe, which basically matched his skin color. "She's following you, trailing you."

I let his words sink in, staring at him like he was crazy. "Are you saying that woman is haunting me?"

Crane opened his mouth, about to refute my haunting statement, but he quickly shut it, pensive. "I would say tracking you, watching you, to see if you're a good fit." When I only stared at him, he went on, "I'm sure the spirits feel you. I'm sure you're a shining beacon in the haze that is the otherworld. You draw them in."

Oh, that's all? Just wonderful.

"It would be easier, I assume, to possess you while your soul is locked in the otherworld than it would be to cross the veil itself, even though it is weakening." Crane ran a hand through his brown hair; since I'd caught him at a bad time, it was not combed how it usually was. Its wavy lengths were messy, kind of cute. "I'll have to do some research, try to figure out who she is before she shows herself to you again."

"And there's no way to kill a spirit?" I asked, blinking, suddenly feeling so very tired. I could lean back and fall asleep on this couch, right here, right now.

Crane pursed his lips. "None that I'm aware of. If a human is possessed, the only way to get the spirit out of the human is to kill the human, and even then…the spirit doesn't die. It simply returns to the otherworld. But once it knows how to cross…"

"It's easier for it to come back to earth," I said, to which he nodded.

"That will be a problem to deal with tomorrow," Crane said, reaching toward my face, fingertips lightly brushing against my cheek. "Let me get something to clean you up with." He stood, heading into the kitchen. When he returned, he carried a small bowl, along with a washcloth.

I watched as he sat beside me, dabbing the tip of the towel in the bowl. I turned my body to face his, inhaling slowly, willing myself to stay up, to not fall over from exhaustion. Not yet, anyway.

"Close your eyes," Crane instructed, and I shut them. He brought the towel to my face, softly rubbing the warm, wet fabric around my right eye. "You will be staying here tonight." Not an offer, not a question, but a command. It was one I would listen to. I didn't feel safe anywhere I went…but with Crane?

I wasn't sure how I felt with Crane.

As he moved to clean the other eye and my cheek, I muttered, "When I came back into myself, I couldn't see for a few moments."

Crane took the towel off my face for a few seconds, and through mostly-closed lids, I was able to see a concerned, anxious expression on his elegant face.

"You had momentary blindness?" he asked, and I nodded, feeling his other hand gently grip my chin to hold me still as he continued cleaning my face. "Your father never experienced any similar symptoms, although he couldn't cross over like you can. How long were you there?"

I shrugged. "Five minutes, maybe."

"That is a while, I would think."

He no longer dabbed at my face, and I heard him set the bowl down on the floor. I kept my eyes closed, mostly because I was sad about it all. I didn't want to be the key to anything. Opening the veil, closing the veil—I didn't want to do shit to the veil. I just wanted to take care of my dad's stuff, have his funeral, and leave Sleepy Hollow.

Leaving Sleepy Hollow seemed further out of reach as the hours ticked by.

"Are you done?" I asked quietly.

"I am, I'm sorry," Crane's voice came quickly, and as I slowly opened my eyes, I found he stared at me. "You're just..." He adjusted his glasses again, a light pink color in his cheeks. "You're the most beautiful woman I've ever seen, so much so that it's hard for me to look at you sometimes, knowing that I..."

The men of Sleepy Hollow were hot and cold. They'd shower me with compliments one moment and leave me in a rage the next. Still, I wanted to know what he was going to say. "That you what?"

His hands rested on his lap, folded over each other in a way that spelled refined. "I can never have you."

I could only stare at him.

"I was never here during the summers when you were here, and I hated it, though when I was younger, I didn't know why," Crane spoke. He was a few years older than me, but not much. Just under thirty, I'd say. "All those years, when my parents would drag us to warmer climates, when I should've been having fun in the sun and all of that, I was lost. My heart remained in Sleepy Hollow, but it wasn't until your father found me and started working with me that I knew why. One day he showed me a picture of you. It was an old picture, but even then, I recognized you."

What he was saying…it sounded remarkably close to what Bones had said. He'd always liked me. Crane was saying he'd liked me too, even before knowing me? Even before meeting me? How was that possible?

This was Sleepy Hollow. The realm of possibility was much larger here than it was anywhere else.

"I've been dying to meet you ever since," Crane admitted, his gaze falling to his lap, acting sheepish, ashamed for admitting these things to me. "I only wish it didn't take your father's death."

I lifted a hand, reaching for him, all the while not knowing what I was doing but doing it anyway. I touched his face, his cheek, drawing my fingers down his gaunt cheekbone and along his jaw.

Why the hell was I touching him? I shouldn't be. This was the stranger that I threatened with a frying pan not too long ago. Crane was not my type—at least, before now, I didn't think he was my type. Now…now I was starting to wonder if I had more than one type.

Two types.

Bones and Crane.

My heart was heavy in my chest, and a part of me wanted to lean into Crane, to latch onto him and have him tell me everything was going to be alright, but I didn't. I couldn't. I dropped my hand from his face, breaking away from his green-eyed stare and muttering, "I'm tired."

Crane coughed. "Of course. Let me take you to one of the guest rooms."

I got up, feeling a bit wobbly but able to walk on my own. We left the bowl and the small towel on the floor as we headed up the steps. Crane brought me to the third floor, to a bedroom with vaulted ceilings and rich, mahogany-carved furniture. I immediately went towards the bed, but Crane hung on the doorframe.

"It's right next to my room, so if something does happen, do not hesitate to shout for me," he said. "Sleep means nothing to me, not when you're distressed." Crane talked like someone out of a different time period half of the time, but nonetheless, his words made me feel comforted.

I crawled into the bed after taking off my boots, tossing him a look before I laid down. "Thank you," I whispered.

Through the darkness, he gave me a small smile. Crane's smiles were not overly eager, nor were they particularly confident. His smile didn't have the dimples behind it to back it up, and yet I found myself drawn to his lips anyway.

"Anything for you," he spoke, pausing a moment, his stare lingering on me for a few seconds before he padded off to his own room.

I sunk in the sheets, resting my head on the large, fluffy pillow under me. I pulled up the sheets to my neck, feeling the strange need to be wrapped in these blankets like a cocoon. I also wanted Crane in here with me, in the same bed as me. Tonight, I didn't want to be alone, but I was.

I was alone, and even though I told myself history was not going to repeat itself for me, it was. I had feelings for Bones, that much was obvious—but similar feelings had begun to bud for Crane, too.

Just like the original Katrina Van Tassel, I was stuck between two men. Well, technically, two men and a Headless Horseman, not to mention a crazy-looking spirit woman who may or may not want to possess me, but I was choosing *not* to include the latter two in my equation. It made me feel a little better.

Chapter Nine

I was slow to open my eyes, spotting the white sky above me. This...was it the otherworld? I sat up, my hands clutching two handfuls of green grass. No, it couldn't be. A big yellow ball sat in the sky, the sun. I was confused though, because there was a haze between the sun and the ground, almost like all of its light couldn't get through.

As I got to my feet, I had the vaguest memory of running through a field like this before...only last time it wasn't covered in bodies. Corpses were strewn all around me, their bodies torn with bullet holes. Each and every body wore the same uniform, all of them men.

I took a step forward, the white dress I wore swaying in the breeze that carried the stale air up to my nostrils. No, I took that back. Not all of them were men. Some were no more than boys, twelve years old, at the most.

This was the cold, hard, ugly truth of war. A war that was held years ago. Centuries. A war that knew no modern guns but muskets and cannons. The carnage was almost too much. I didn't want to look at it. Some girls were fascinated with death and swooned over those serial killer documentaries on Netflix, but I was not one of them.

I hated death. I hated the blood. And, above all else, I hated how the air reeked with the smell of rotting flesh and maggots.

I recognized the field we were in. It was one in Sleepy Hollow, just off the square, where the old-timey shops were. It was where war reenactments were held during the summer, apparently right over the buried bones of these people.

Something took hold of my heart, squeezing it, refusing to let it beat naturally, and I turned my head, spotting someone else standing in the field, amongst the bodies. My breath caught in my throat. It was him.

The Headless Horseman.

He stood, at least fifty feet away, his wide, impressive chest rising and falling with breaths he should not be able to take. His gloved hands were fisted at his sides, and for a while, we were both frozen, both staring at each other. I mean, I assumed he stared at me.

Kind of difficult to tell when he had no head and no eyes.

His right hand slowly extended, his fingers suddenly grasping the handle of a shimmering, reddish ax. In one swift movement, he jerked the ax down, severing the head of the nearest corpse. Still clutching the ax in one hand, he used his other to pick up the head and throw it at me.

The head rolled against my feet, and I leaped back, feeling the need to vomit. It wasn't bleeding anymore, but I think a bleeding head might've been better. This one, a middle-aged man with a long, greying beard, was full of crawling maggots in his eyes and nose, not to mention the wriggling things in his mouth... The skin was black and blue, and I gagged.

No. No, no, no.

I looked up, frowning, realizing that the Headless Horseman had started to come closer, his huge body hulking like a giant. He still held onto his ax, and before I knew what I was doing, I turned, sprinting away.

I would not let him reach me. I would not let him get to me. I wouldn't—

I needn't have bothered to try, apparently, because suddenly he was in front of me, and I skidded to a halt, mere inches away from his chest. This was not going to end well for me. Sheer panic set in, and as I tried to turn away to try to run again, he grabbed my wrist, stopping me.

Why did he have to be so strong? Why was he always there? Why couldn't he just let me go?

"I'm sorry," I said, crying out as he dragged me closer, his grip on my wrist too hard. So tight it cut off the circulation in my hand. I couldn't escape him, and even when I dug my feet into the ground, I couldn't stop him from pulling me back to him.

Somehow he'd gotten another head, and as he held my wrist with a grip so strong it could break bones, he shoved the newly severed head in my face.

I winced, looking away from the dried-up eyes of the head, but the Headless Horseman yanked on my wrist, wanting me to look at it. Why? Why torture me like this? Why not just end it here and kill me?

He must've been angry, for he threw down the head, released my wrist and grabbed my head with a force that threatened to crush my skull. His hands were large, his gloved fingers nearly encircling my entire skull. His impossibly wide chest heaved with a rage-filled breath, and I was lost. I didn't know what to do.

Was this it? Was I going to die right now, in the hands of the Headless Horseman? I didn't want to die.

Just when I started to wonder what death was going to feel like, the force around my head lifted, and he moved a hand down my neck, trailing his well-beaten leather glove to my chest, pointing...at me?

My heart threatened to burst. Was he...trying to communicate with me?

The hand whose finger touched my chest, directly above the area where my heart was, sluggishly moved off, and then he pointed to himself. Tap, tap, tap, he kept pressing his finger against his chest, as if I'd understand what he was trying to say.

"I don't..." My words came out in a rush, and I glanced up, temporarily forgetting who was before me. Headless. No eyes to gaze up in. No head to see what expression he wore. Nothing to help me tell whether he was angry at me or what. Angry, or pleading, or desperate.

The world around us grew brighter, the sky suddenly changing and becoming blue. The sun's rays intensified, and I squinted, feeling the strange sensation of disappearing. The Headless Horseman grabbed my arm, trying to stop me from going, but even his iron grip couldn't stop me from waking up from the dream.

A dream.

It was all a dream.

A dream in the otherworld? I'd have to ask Crane about it.

I blinked my eyes open and was greeted with sunlight streaming through the windows on the other side of the room. Despite how freaky that dream was, I actually felt refreshed. I rolled out of bed, stretching. Leaving my boots at the base of the bed, I tiptoed toward the bedroom next door, figuring Crane was still asleep since I didn't hear any other noises in the house.

Crane slept in a king-sized bed, his arms splayed out on the pillow beside his head. His glasses sat on the nightstand, and as I crept closer, being as quiet as I could, I found myself smiling. His brown hair was even messier than it was last night, his mouth open just a bit. No snoring, which was good.

Not sure why I thought it was good, because I wasn't going to ever spend the night with him, but...

All of my thoughts trailed off as I moved to the edge of the bed, gazing down at him, a softness in my heart. Almost as if I cared for him—which was crazy. I didn't care for him. The feelings his words and closeness had stirred in me last night were...in no way real.

There was no way I could've fallen for a guy as strange as Crane so fast. No fucking way. Unless magic was involved, I couldn't like him...

I didn't.

I wouldn't.

I…I did.

Moving until I sat on the bed, I stretched a hand out towards his sleeping figure, hesitating but needing to touch him. An innate pull towards him, something I couldn't fight. His face was a bit prickly with stubble, but beyond that, Crane was perfect. A pale, perfect, slightly kooky sleeping angel.

I leaned my head closer, my auburn hair draping down off my shoulders. My fingertips touched his chin, all of my focus on his mouth. What did I come in here for? Why was I practically crawling on top of him like he was mine to have whenever I wanted? I couldn't wake him up with a kiss…but holy hell, did I want to.

Would it be so bad, though, if I did? Would he freak out and slap me in the face?

My head was less than five inches from his, my hand on his neck when his emerald gaze peeked open. I had no idea how good his vision was without his glasses, and I stumbled over excuses in my head, wondering how the hell I was going to play this one off.

I shouldn't have worried so much.

Crane lifted his head up to mine, finding my mouth with ease. His kiss was a slow one, tentative and unsure at first. He moaned a bit into the kiss, and when his hands found my back, I let him pull me down towards him completely. Somehow my body wound up under the sheets, on top of his.

His hands tangled in my hair, tugging gently as his kisses grew to be more fervent, hungrier, more eager. I straddled him, feeling an erection pressing against me between my legs. My hips dug against it, rubbing my jeans over his boxers. He was, I realized as I trailed my hands down his chest, shirtless. Crane was lean, but he wasn't without muscles. He wasn't nearly as lanky as I thought he was when I first saw him.

The moment I started to rub myself against his hardness, Crane flipped us, laying me down on his pillow, basking in his warmth and his scent as his mouth demolished mine. His hands ran all over me, cupping my breasts, kneading them with vigor. My legs wrapped around him, and just when I was about to suggest we get rid of the rest of our clothes, Crane tore his lips off mine and stared at me for a moment.

He blinked again and again, one of his hands still cupping my breasts. The pressure between his hard-on, which had started to escape his boxers, and myself lessened. "Kat?" Crane asked, his voice husky. "Oh, dear. I'm…I'm so sorry. I didn't—" He practically flew off me, like I had the plague or something.

With his back to me, he reached for his glasses, flexing the hand that had been so recently cupped against my left boob. I was still out of breath, still clueless at the switch. He was going along with it so well before he suddenly decided he didn't want to kiss me anymore.

"That was wholly inappropriate, and I'm sorry," he apologized again, glancing back at me, his green eyes lucid and clear behind his glasses. His hands were on his lap, probably trying to hide his erection from me.

I leaned towards him, setting a hand on his bare back. His shoulders were a lot nicer than his slim frame would suggest. His skin trembled beneath my touch, and I moved closer, kneeling beside him on the bed, watching as his cheeks burned pink. "Why are you apologizing?" I asked. "You weren't the one who started it." My eyes were on his mouth, his lips a bit pinker than they usually were. "I did."

And I wanted to keep going, too…but he was right. Now wasn't the time for that. I had to tell him about my dream.

"Oh…uh," Crane paused, seemingly awkward once he noticed my gaze was on his mouth, "is there a reason why?"

How could I tell him that I was drawn to him like a helpless moth toward the flame? I didn't even know why I did it, so trying to find the correct words to explain it to him without sounding nuts would be impossible.

Wait a minute. This was Crane I was talking to. He and nuts went hand in hand.

"I feel drawn to you," I murmured, practically swooning over his bare back.

"But you didn't feel the same the first time you saw me?" When I was silent, realizing he was right, Crane got to his feet, leaving me alone in his bed. "Your connection to Sleepy Hollow is growing at a rapid pace. If I didn't know any better, I'd say this town wants us to have a repeat of the original tale."

Was he saying I didn't like him? Was he saying the connection I felt with him was merely because of Sleepy Hollow? I didn't know what to make of it, but I knew I didn't like it. My feelings were my own… weren't they?

I mean, a man like Crane—he wasn't the kind of guy you tripped over your feet for. His cuteness was the kind that snuck up on you, a nerdy kind of cute. When I'd first met him, I found him rifling through my dad's things; of course I was going to be upset with him. To say everything I felt toward him was just because of this stupid town was asinine.

I got off the bed, hurrying toward his side. He was in the closet, a walk-in closet because he was stinking rich, choosing a shirt and some pants. He had the pants on already, his hard-on tucked up into the waistline of his boxers, but not zipped up. Not yet. And no shirt yet, either.

"No," I said, moving before him. I tore the shirt out of his hands, probably wrinkling it too much, since it was one of those nice, button-up ones. "You're wrong."

Crane's head tilted down, a look of exasperation on his face. "It's okay, Kat. I know I'm not...your type. You'd rather spend your time with a man like Brom, and I don't blame you. I'm not like him—"

God, I bet he could go on and on, putting himself down for ages.

I shut him up by stepping closer, wrapping an arm around his neck and pulling his tall frame down to mine, bringing my mouth to his. Not nearly as heated of a kiss as the ones we had on the bed, but this wasn't about that. This was to show him that my feelings were real.

At least, I hoped they were. I'd feel like a huge idiot if they weren't.

"Stop it," I said, breaking the kiss. He'd been too shocked at my forwardness to do much else besides take the kiss. "Don't compare yourself to Bones." If Crane would stop and think, stop and take a quick look around, he'd realize that I wasn't with Bones right now. I was with him, in his house. Bones had stormed out of here, so angry last night, and I...

Damn it, I wasn't happy with him. Such a hypocrite about the supernatural.

My eyes fell to his abdomen, where a trail of dark hair ran from his belly button downward, disappearing beneath the hem of his boxers, which I could still see since his pants were not zipped up yet. "Now get dressed. There's something we have to talk about." I left him in the closet, heading downstairs.

I was lost in the kitchen. I wanted to make coffee, to do something, but all I ended up doing was peeking in every single drawer and cabinet until Crane came down, effortlessly knowing what I wanted. He pulled out some coffee grains and started making it for me. He would, of course, have more tea.

Once we were both seated on barstools, with our respective drinks on the counter before us, I heaved a giant breath and started to tell him my dream. Everything about it. I didn't leave out a single detail, knowing Crane needed the whole story. All the while I wondered if he would think the same thing I did.

Once I was finished, Crane processed everything I said. His brown hair was still a bit messy, and I resisted my urge to run my fingers through it. Crane was still freaked out about what happened between us, so I'd lay off, for now.

"It does sound like he is trying to communicate with you," Crane relented, his shoulders moving up and down in a sigh. "But he's been a spirit for so long, I think he's lost touch with how to communicate nicely."

I managed to chuckle. The sound drew Crane's gaze, but I pretended not to notice. "He wasn't always a spirit?"

"He is one of the rarer cases," Crane spoke, pausing to take a sip out of his mug. "A human who perished in an awful way, trapped in the otherworld, unfinished business keeping him around."

"I thought you said humans weren't spirits?" Or was it that ghosts weren't spirits? All the nitty-gritty shit; I wasn't a fan of it, but when it came down to the Headless Horseman, I had to know.

"I said ghosts were not real," Crane said, a delicateness to his tone I didn't appreciate. Like I was a newbie to all of this. I mean, I was, but I didn't want to be treated like one. "Legend says the Headless Horseman was decapitated by a cannonball sometime during the Revolutionary War, and he's in constant search of his head, which he just can't seem to find."

Crane and I both realized it at the same time, our gazes locking. "You don't think…"

"He's asking you to find his head," he whispered. "Perhaps. I don't think he's ever asked someone before—or maybe he has, and they couldn't understand, so he simply killed them and waited for someone else who would help him. He's roamed the otherworld of Sleepy Hollow for centuries in search of it."

Helping the Headless Horseman find his head…why did I feel like that wasn't all of it?

I was about to voice my suspicions, but my phone rang. I dug it out of my pocket, finding that it was nearly dead. I recognized the number as Mike, my dad's lawyer. Finally. Holding up a finger, I slid off the stool and answered it. "Mike? I've been trying to reach you for days—"

"Yes," Mike answered, "I've been...busy." His voice sounded stilted, almost like a robot. That, or he really wasn't a morning person. "I can meet with you in thirty minutes at my office. Does that work for you?"

"Sure," I said, wanting to get it over with as quickly as possible. I wasn't sure how long the local hospital would hold my dad's body, but I knew not forever. He gave me the address to his office and hung up.

I met Crane's stare, and Crane asked, "You have to go?"

"My dad's lawyer."

Nodding once, Crane got up and grabbed a set of keys. "I'll drive you."

I went upstairs and got my boots. As we left his house, I couldn't help but feel a nagging pinch in my gut. Not a good feeling. Something that told me this thing with the Headless Horseman wasn't over, and that I was not only connected to Sleepy Hollow, Crane, and Bones, but also the headless man himself. And that said nothing about what happened to my dad...if a spirit had been the cause of his death, to bring me back here.

I inhaled, exhaling slowly, drawing out the breath as we headed further into town.

One thing at a time.

Chapter Ten

The lawyer's office was in one of the shops on the main street of Sleepy Hollow. If you were to walk by it without knowing what it was, you'd never suspect it was where the town's few lawyers set up shop. I waved goodbye to Crane, who reassured me that he was going to investigate the white-haired woman and the Headless Horseman. He also suggested I return to his house after the meeting, which I was slightly inclined to agree to, mostly because walking around out here, I had no idea when I was going to be thrown into the otherworld again.

I headed into the office, greeted by a secretary who was on the phone. She saw me, pointed down the hall, her wordless way of telling me to go right in.

The place was old, taken straight out of one of those cop movies. The walls had wooden pressboard on them, the lights dim and yellow. Mike's office sat behind a closed door, the small glass square on the door frosted with his name in big, black letters.

I knocked, finding the door creaked open. Sticking my head in, I found Mike sitting at a desk full of papers. The man wore a suit that had seen better days, and a tie that looked like it had some stains on it. He was an older man, maybe early sixties, one of the too-serious types. Not exactly the kind of lawyer I would've pegged for my dad.

"Hi Mike, I'm Kat, Phil's daughter." I reached out a hand to shake his, but he only glanced up at me. He didn't offer to shake, didn't even get up. His dark eyes only flicked to the seat opposite him, so I simply sat down, feeling immensely and immediately awkward.

Mike grunted as he got up, moving to close the door. Right. Privacy and all that. He lumbered back to his leather chair, moving as if he weighed five hundred pounds instead of the hundred and seventy-five he probably did. He moved slowly, deliberately, almost like he had to stop and think about what to do.

Hmm. He was weird. Maybe that's why my dad had him as his lawyer.

I stared at Mike for a while, waiting for him to pull out a folder with my dad's name on it, or something. I wasn't sure what lawyers did, but I was fairly sure they weren't supposed to just sit there and stare at you. Unless my breath smelled that bad? I hadn't exactly had my morning routine today, since I woke up at Crane's…

"Uh," I broke the silence, leaning forward, trying to see if one of the many papers on his desk was my dad's will, which we had to go over. "Maybe we should start off with the will?" I suggested with a shrug, not wanting to push this guy's buttons.

For one, the buttons on his shirt and suit were probably at least two decades old. Secondly, the way he stared at me—one step down from outright glaring—made me a teeny, tiny bit uncomfortable.

Okay, a lot uncomfortable.

I met Mike's eyes, and for a split, impossibly fast second, all I saw were the whites. But then I blinked again, and they were back to normal. I said nothing, reaching into my pocket to pull out my phone. Officially dead now, of course. Why would the battery have lasted just a few minutes longer?

I slowly slid my phone back into my pocket, watching as Mike's lips twisted into a frown. He opened his mouth, revealing teeth that were far too yellow and old…teeth that appeared just a tad sharper than they should've been.

Shit. This guy was possessed? I had to get out of here, now.

Lurching to my feet, I turned toward the door, about to make a run for it, but I was no longer in the real world. When I turned, I turned right into the otherworld. My exit was blocked by a huge, lumbering figure who could tower over even the tallest of people.

It was him. Of course it was him. Who else would it be? So tall, so wide, so fucking headless.

He stood not even five feet from me, between me and my exit, and I watched his intimidating figure take a step closer to me.

I glanced over my shoulder, finding Mike's seat was empty. We were alone in this room, in the slightly off-colored otherworld. Just me and the Headless Horseman. Two buddies reuniting.

His wide chest tilted somewhat, and I imagined him cocking his head at me, studying me in the same manner I studied him. What did he think of me, I wondered, just a frightened woman? Someone in over their head? Had he seen the original Katrina, and did he know I was her lookalike?

He took a step towards me, and then another, and another. I found myself nearly tripping over my own feet as I stumbled back, my ass leaning on the table.

Everything was just a bit hazy, and I hoped I wouldn't get sent back into the real world blind again. Not while I was stuck with Mike and whatever spirit was inside of him.

The Headless Horseman moved to stand between me and the chair I'd been sitting in, his body mere inches away from pinning me against the desk.

"I…" I hated how weak my voice sounded. This man, this spirit, this giant-like creature, whatever he was, he made me nervous. And scared. And whatever other adjective I could use to describe the tumultuous feelings inside of me. "I know what you want."

His chest rose and fell with a single, deep breath, the gloved hands at his sides clenching, the sound of tightening leather filling up the silence of the room.

"You want your head," I added.

He sluggishly lifted a hand, shoving a finger against my chest, nearly pushing me down on the desk with the amount of force he used. That would definitely bruise—or at least it would if this was the real world. I still was unsure of how most of this stuff worked. All of this was new to me, and still scarier than I wanted to admit.

Dealing with the Headless Horseman...who would've imagined he was real, let alone truly haunting the old bridge in Sleepy Hollow?

The finger left my chest, and he pointed at himself. Now that I knew what he was after, I wasn't as confused as I was in my dream. Hell, I still had no idea how he'd been able to slip in my dreams to begin with. But just because I wasn't as confused did not mean I wasn't as frightened.

This man...he could kill me with his pinky. He could heave a thunderous breath with his wide chest and knock me off my feet. I felt like a child standing in front of him, small and useless, weak and simply not enough.

If I helped him, if I helped the Headless Horseman find his head, what would that do for me? Would he leave me alone? Would he let me be, or would he simply kill me afterward? Would he go on to terrorize Sleepy Hollow with his newfound head, or would he give up the hauntings? I wanted to ask him these things, desperately needing answers to them, but seeing as how he had no mouth, there were no lips to form the words I wanted to hear.

"You want me to help you find your head," I whispered, pushing myself off the side of the table. I might be cowering in my boots, but I was not going to act like it. No, I would suck it up and face down this legendary man and his headless figure, even if his headless form was something out of a fairy tale.

I mean, no one was that large, were they? Tall people were usually lanky, kind of like Crane. But this guy…underneath his uniform, he had muscles for days. His figure, the way he steadily breathed in and out even without a head, was what helped make him so utterly terrifying.

The hand pointing to himself dropped, and he must not have liked my *taking a stand* stance. The Headless Horseman stepped closer, his double-sided ax forming in his hands, non-corporeal and incomplete, as if the ax itself faded in and out of existence. My ass leaned against the desk behind me, and I felt his masculine form press against me. He was solid beneath his uniform, but I felt no warmth coming off him, no body heat.

I froze as I watched him raise his ax. Was this it? Was he done with me? Was he through waiting for me to agree to help him finally end the centuries-long search for his head? I closed my eyes, not wanting to see it coming.

Or maybe I should look.

My eyes peeked open when I felt a rush of air near my head, but when I opened them, the world around me was no more. Or, rather, the world was black. I couldn't see.

I fell forward, falling on my knees as I tried to find the chair I'd been sitting in before all of this happened. I forced myself to blink over and over again, knowing that each second I wasted blind was another second that Mike could hop over his desk and kill me. Or do whatever the hell he wanted to me.

My vision returned to me as I crawled up, pulling myself into the chair. I spun, breathing hard as tears of blood seeped from my eyes. As it turned out, I needn't have worried about what Mike was going to do to me. You might be wondering why, or you might already know.

Mike was dead, his chest torn apart, a thick, gory red line seeping out of his clothes, as if someone threw an ax right at him. His head hung back, his mouth open. His dark eyes were normal, no extra milky white parts to them. Mike was dead, no longer possessed, and the spirit who'd been inside him was thrown back to the otherworld…but it wouldn't be for long. Who knew how long it would take for that spirit to return and find me again. What if it possessed Crane next? Or Bones?

I was going to be sick.

I wiped the bloody tears from my face, practically leaping out of the chair to run into the hall. I stumbled on my own feet until I rammed myself against the receptionist's desk. She was still on the phone, but once saw me, she said, "Frank, I'm going to have to call you back." And then she hung up, her stare meeting mine.

"Call the police," I said. I thought about saying there's been a murder, but stopped short. While it was true, it was…well, the only person in the room with Mike while he'd been alive was me, and I really didn't want to be put under investigation while I was here. Not that I had anything to hide, but…

Shit. This made everything so much more complicated.

As the receptionist got up, needing to see for herself just what I meant, I lumbered for one of the chairs in the hallway. A makeshift seating room for other clients while they waited. Mike would have no more clients anymore. What did that mean about my dad? His will? How long would it take to get a new lawyer? Or maybe I could just go in there and take it?

The receptionist's high-pitched scream echoed down the hall, and she ran out of Mike's office, looking much paler than she did moments ago. I met her questioning eyes, saying nothing as I pointed to the phone.

The cops. I needed the cops.

In particular, one cop. I needed Bones, and I needed to convince him that I wasn't crazy.

Chapter Eleven

The police clearly didn't know what to make of it. The whole thing confused them, made one of them look a particularly bad kind of nauseous, and all the while I sat there in the hallway, until one of them hauled me in and took me to the station, where I sat in a white room, alone and waiting. I knew it was only a matter of time until Bones showed his face. He wouldn't leave me in here for long. He'd hear about what happened at the lawyer's place, what happened to the lawyer, and then he'd come rushing in, wanting to save the day. Wanting to save me.

At least, I hoped so.

As I sat there, staring at the metal table in front of me, the hard coolness of the chair beneath me chilling my back, I started to worry he wouldn't. He wasn't thrilled when he stormed out of Crane's; what if he metaphorically washed his hands of me? What if Bones was finally, after all these years, done with me? If this was the last straw…

Just as I was thinking that depressing thought, the door to the interrogation room opened, and the man of the hour walked in, carrying a steaming cup of coffee, which he set in front of me before taking the seat opposite mine. Bones looked…tired. There weren't dark bags beneath his eyes, but he looked exhausted all the same, blonde scruff on his chin, his hair flat as if he hadn't yet washed it today.

Still beyond sexy, but that was beside the point. I'd basically just witnessed a murder, of which I was probably the only suspect. Now was not the time to daydream about Bones. There'd be plenty of time for that later.

"You want to tell me what happened in there?" Bones asked, his deep voice soothing, settling in my core, a calming warmth that made me instantly relax. "Because from what I hear, it's not good."

Bones hadn't been one of the first responders, but seeing as how that happened hours ago, he had plenty of time to get himself caught up. I went into Mike's office, I left Mike's office, Mike was dead. That's it. Pretty simple.

"Am I being arrested?" I asked, totally avoiding the question. I asked mainly because I didn't want to be arrested...then again, when I came to this town to pack up my dad's things, sell his house and arrange a funeral for him, I didn't want to linger longer than I had to in Sleepy Hollow. Yet here I was, knee-deep in shit. Didn't look like I'd be leaving this place any time soon.

My heart ached in my chest when Bones's blue gaze held my stare. A growing part of me didn't want to leave town; it wanted to explore whatever strange feelings I had for him, and for Crane.

Caught in a love triangle just like the original Katrina Van Tassel. My dad would be so proud.

"No," Bones said, leaning back in the chair. The dark fabric across his chest grew taut, and even though it was a button-down shirt, I could still see the outline of his muscles. "But you might be, depending on what happens. There is a dead body, Kat. We don't take things like that lightly here."

"I didn't kill him."

"I don't think you did, either. We're just trying to figure out what happened in there. The receptionist said you went back, and then, not even ten minutes later, he was dead." Bones heaved a sigh. "You can see how things don't exactly look good for you."

"We were alone in the room," I said, biting my bottom lip to stop myself from bringing up the Headless Horseman. Bones might've grown up in Sleepy Hollow, but like Crane said—believing in the local superstitions was vastly different than believing real, genuine spirits haunted the town.

Bones studied me. "How did Mike wind up with a foot-long gash in his chest?"

Ugh. So much for not bringing up the Headless Horseman, huh? Seemed that bastard followed me wherever I went. Literally.

"An ax," I spoke delicately, as if speaking of murder was a normal thing for me. Newsflash: it wasn't. The only thing keeping me sane right now was the fact that Mike probably would've killed me, or worse, if the Headless Horseman hadn't done what he did. The damned guy saved me. I…I guess I owed him one.

"An ax?" Bones asked, cocking his head. I could see the gears working behind his eyes, and I knew he wasn't getting it.

"You didn't find the murder weapon in the room because," I paused, feeling dread coat every part of me, "it was his."

"Mike's?" Bones had the wrong idea, clearly. "You're saying Mike did this to himself?"

"I'm saying," I lowered my voice, glancing at the camera in the upper corner of the room, at the blinking red light that told me it recorded everything that went on in this room. I didn't want to sound nuts, not like my dad. He might've been the town crazy, but I wasn't about to fill his shoes. "Something else did it."

Bones's expression fell.

"I know how crazy it is," I said, my back hunching toward the table. The coffee sat untouched in front of me. "But it's true. Compare the wound with axes. A weapon that size? I probably couldn't even lift it, let alone throw it across the desk and practically cleave someone in two." I doubted even Bones would be that strong. The Headless Horseman was...on his own level.

The fucking god-tier.

Bones took his time in saying, "The wound was...cauterized."

Cauterized? My eyebrows came together. "Doesn't that mean—"

"It means whatever killed him was either really hot, or…" Bones trailed off. "Fuck. I don't know, Kat. I don't know what it means. I know I said things are weird here, but this? This is murder."

"So you'll play off breaking and entering to ghosts, but not murder?"

His azure stare lingered on me, a muscle in his jaw clenching. "A gust of wind could've blown through a window you didn't know was open—"

"And tossed around wooden drawers?" I knew my voice rose with each breath, and I took another deep one to calm myself. Getting angry at Bones wouldn't help. I had to make him see what I saw, to make him understand that this wasn't some crazy conspiracy…but how?

Crane. Crane would have to help with that.

"You know I didn't do it," I said, calmer this time.

"I know," he whispered, and then proceeded to stare at me, pensive.

We sat like that for a long while, each of us lost in our own heads until Bones got up and left the room. *Well, I guess I'll just make myself as comfortable as I can here, considering it doesn't look like I'll be leaving anytime soon.*

After what felt like hours, another officer came in. This time, it was the pretty woman who I'd seen talking to Bones before. She wore a frown when she looked at me, but even then, she was pretty. Flawless skin, slightly curled hair, nice boobs. Bones would be so much better off with her than with me. I…I don't know why, but at least if he was with her, it would make things so much easier. No more tug-o-war going on in my soul.

"Write down exactly what happened," the woman said, passing me a pen and a notebook.

My official statement. I had no idea how to make it sound less loony and more realistic, but I'd do my best. I started jotting down what happened, pretending to ignore the way the woman stared at me. I couldn't help but wonder if she thought I was crazy. Like father, like daughter, right? The apple didn't fall too far from the tree and all that. Or maybe she actually thought I'd done the murdering myself.

I decided on saying that I'd blacked out—not totally a lie—and fallen out of the chair I was in while I panicked. I didn't hear anything, didn't see anything. When I came to, Mike was dead. It was true enough. These cops didn't have evidence besides me being the only one in the room. A big weapon like that—you couldn't hide it in your pants or tuck it away for next time. An ax that size was impossible to hide, and it was obvious I wasn't strong. They couldn't pin this on me.

After I finished, she took my statement and left me alone in the room again. I twiddled my thumbs for what felt like forever before Bones returned, holding the door open for me. He said nothing, his blonde head gesturing for me to get up and follow him, so I did. I got up, moving to his side, trailing after him as he led me down the hall.

"You're not to leave town while the investigation is underway," Bones said, glancing at me. "The chief didn't want to release you, but I told him I'd keep an eye on you, make sure you don't leave Sleepy Hollow."

So I owed my release today to Bones. I was surprised, considering how mad he was at Crane's, but I guess I shouldn't be.

He brought me to the front of the station, stopping right before the doors. Outside, the world was sunny, as if it had no idea that a murder took place earlier. Weather never cooperated. I glanced outside for a split-second before lifting my gaze to his. I opened my mouth to say something, anything, but Bones stopped me.

"Don't," he said. "I just…I know you have to deal with Phil's stuff, so go. Do what you have to do. I'll keep you updated." Something passed behind his eyes, and I refrained from asking him what was wrong.

There…was a lot wrong here. To ask would be stupid.

"Thank you," I said, leaving it at that as I exited the station. The wind immediately lapped at my skin, and I ran my hands along my arms, fighting the chill that instantly swept over me. It was as if this town knew it had me in its clutches and refused to let me go.

I headed through town, heading straight to Crane's house. It took me ages to walk up his long driveway, even longer to muster up the courage to use the metal door knocker on the elegant front door. Crane and Bones didn't like each other; I had no idea whether or not Crane would help me at all, but I had to try. I couldn't stand Bones being mad, and I hated the notion that he thought me just as insane as my dad. Everyone here might've loved my dad, but I was certain behind his back, the insults flew.

Crane answered the door in a few minutes, blinking wildly behind his thin-rimmed glasses. He'd showered recently, his short brown hair sticking up a bit. His tall, lean frame wore new, pressed clothes. He looked like a model taken straight out of a clothing catalog, which was a ridiculous comparison to make, but it was true.

I would say he looked silly, but somehow, someway, Crane pulled the clothes off. The only thing he looked was good.

"Kat," he spoke my name softly. "How did it go?"

"How did what go?" I asked, sounding quite dumb. It was as I spoke that I remembered the day's events. Meeting with Mike, realizing Mike was possessed, seeing the Headless Horseman, coming back to the real world to view a dead Mike. It was a doozy of a day. Before Crane could say anything else, I pushed past him, heading inside.

There's a lot we needed to talk about.

Chapter Twelve

Crane understood how important it was to clear my name or the murder—or at least have Bones on my side. If we had him believing in this stuff, if we helped to open his eyes to the supernatural world surrounding Sleepy Hollow, maybe he could help steer the investigation another direction, or even close it. I knew I was the last person to see Mike alive, and I knew there was no evidence of anyone else in the room, but that's just it. There was no other evidence. They had no leads, and like I'd said, there was no way I could've hidden a giant fucking ax in my pants as I walked by the receptionist or threw it so hard it lodged itself deep inside of him.

Just…no.

Crane had made me tea, which I refused to drink. Mostly because, as I sat there in his extravagant living room, my ass on a couch that probably cost a few thousand dollars, as I stared at the paintings of Sleepy Hollow on the walls, it suddenly hit me.

Yeah, I know. It all hit me a little late, but better late than never, right?

Mike was dead. An innocent man was dead because of me. And it had to be because of me; like Crane said, I was connected to this town somehow. I had no idea what the spirit possessing Mike would've done with me had it taken me, and now we'd never know because the Headless Horseman had killed him. He swung his ax in the otherworld and somehow wound up killing Mike in the real world.

Crane set his cup down, reaching for me. He was about to touch my hands, which were folded on my lap as I stared holes into the carpet, wondering why the hell my life had gotten so messed up, but then he stopped himself, settling for resting a hand on my back. Hesitation after what happened earlier, I suppose, but I was too lost in my own mind to really think about it.

"Kat," Crane spoke my name with a refined delicacy, as if it was the most important word he'd ever say in his life. "We will figure this out. I'll do a bit of digging, go through your father's study again—"

Right. Because he and my dad were working on a bunch of things revolving around spirits and the otherworld, and the veil that was weakening. Whatever. I guess my dad had a thousand different projects going, but he never completed any of them.

Which, honestly, was just great. If I couldn't get Bones to believe me, then...I didn't know what I'd do.

"And what if it doesn't help?" I asked, turning my head to look at him. Crane's green eyes sparkled behind his glasses, his thin lips caught in a semi-frown. Even then, I found him strangely appealing, attractive in a proper, regal way. You know the air people had about them when they had money? Crane had it, and a part of me hated it because I was never a fan of the rich type, but Crane wasn't snobby. He was surprisingly normal, considering.

"It will," he said.

"What if I get locked up for murder?"

"You won't."

"How can you be so sure? Crane, I saw someone die." I paused, thinking back. "Okay, I didn't so much see him die as I did come back to reality and find that he was dead after being blind for a few minutes, but still. Dead. Of course the police think it's me. I was the only one there!" My voice steadily grew louder until it cracked at the end. Being a suspect for murder? Not something on my bucket list.

Then again, I never wanted to come back to Sleepy Hollow either, and here I was. Here I was, wrapped up in a bunch of shit I grew up wanting nothing to do with.

Crane grabbed me by the shoulders, forcing me to meet his eyes. He was a stern kind of serious when he said, "You are not going to be arrested. I will do everything in my power to help you, do you understand? I won't let you take the fall for something a spirit did."

I fought my urge to lean against his shoulders, to close my eyes and breathe him in. With his hands on me, feeling his heat through the fabric of my shirt...let's just say it wasn't helping my case too much. It was ten times harder holding back when we were so close, his arms the only thing holding me up.

"Not just a spirit," I said. "The Headless Horseman." A new thought came to me, and it was a terrible thought, something that made my gut clench in horror and my heart nearly stop. "How long until that spirit finds its way back to this world?" Crane had said once a spirit knows where the veil is thin, it can find it again.

"We have time," Crane said. "A few days, I think. It should be plenty of time to find a solution to this—" AKA help Bones see the spirit-infested light.

"What if it possesses someone else? What if the Headless Horseman just goes around killing them over and over?" My breath caught, and it took ages for me to whisper, "What if it possesses you, or Bones?"

A slow, small smile spread on Crane's lips. The hands gripping my shoulders loosened, falling down to my upper arms, not letting me go completely. A slow, tentative movement that made me shiver. "Spirits take the easy bodies, those whose minds are weak. As much as I'm not a fan of Brom, he's not weak." A moment before he added in a hushed whisper, "And neither am I."

Our gazes locked, and whereas my heart had nearly stopped before, now it sped up, beating so fast it threatened to pop out of my chest. The mere thought of a spirit taking either Crane or Bones was not something I wanted to think about, because of these stupid feelings. As much as I wanted to fight it, I was connected to them both.

Katrina Van Tassel 2.0, new and improved, a modern woman caught in a fucking love triangle. I thought love triangles were a thing of fiction, something you only encountered in books. You know, kind of like those reverse harems that were all the rage now. I mean, multiple guys in love with the same girl?

What were the odds of that happening? And don't even get me started on men being able to share a woman…

Even though I wanted to fall into his chest and press my lips on his, I pulled away, getting up and moving to the closest painting hanging on the wall. It was one of the middle of town, where the town's festivals were held. But it was done before the shops had been built around it; there was nothing but the wooden gazebo and trees in the painting. Hyper-realistic in the way that each leaf had been painted individually. I couldn't imagine how much time that took.

Crane was slow to get up, shoving his hands in his pockets as he moved beside me. He didn't stand too close, but still. I couldn't look at him. "I think it would be best if you stayed here," he said. "This house is warded against spirits, so they won't be able to get to you while you're here. Anywhere you go in town, you shouldn't go alone." Basically he was saying he'd stick to me like glue.

I…was more okay with that than I should've been.

Dumb feelings. Stupid crush. Fucking spirits. Had to go and ruin everything, didn't they?

I sighed, closing my eyes momentarily as I muttered, "You're right."

Who the hell was I trying to kid, anyway? It wasn't like I could go back to my dad's house and continue going through his stuff like nothing had happened. And who knew what was going on with his will, who was in charge of Mike's clients now that Mike was dead. *Wonder how long the hospital will hold onto Dad's body...*

"I'm right?" Crane echoed faintly, bringing me out of my rambling mind. I shot him an annoyed glare, finding that he stared at me with confusion. "Did you just agree with me?" He apparently found the thought of me agreeing with him so farfetched that he needed me to repeat myself. The bastard.

Despite the circumstances, I let out a laugh. "I think I did," I said, shrugging.

"Oh. Well, I was prepared to have to convince you," Crane went on. "That, or tie you up to keep you from marching out there unawares—" His voice halted the moment I stepped closer to him, tilting my head.

I shouldn't be approaching him like this, but here I was, unable to stop myself.

"I didn't know you were the type, Crane," I whispered, a grin spreading on my lips.

His eyes fell to my mouth, watching the smile form as he stuttered, "The—the type to what?" Such a naive, innocent man. Hadn't acted so innocent this morning, though. The way he took charge, it was so unlike him, almost like there were two people inside Crane. One was refined, proper, the kind of man who you'd think would faint at the sight of blood. The other, ironically, had a bit of a dominant streak.

"To tie someone up," I murmured, a calmness sweeping through me as I breathed him in. I wasn't sure what he smelled like, but he smelled good. Or maybe that was just my body needing its release. Maybe I just needed to let off a bit of steam, to really get my mind away from everything else that was going on…

"*Oh*," he said, his pale cheeks flushing. Crane, who had to be around thirty years old, was blushing like a schoolboy who'd been approached by a girl for the first time. Although, from what he'd said before, he had never been interested in other girls growing up. Even though he'd never met me before, he knew me. He felt me. Almost like he was made for me.

I didn't believe in destiny, didn't believe in fate, but what else could I call this? How else could I explain the undeniable feelings inside of me when it came to Crane and Bones? I'd had boyfriends, I'd dated, but none of them really drew my attention, at least not for long. Was this why? Was it because I was supposed to choose between Crane and Bones, just like the original Katrina?

That was the thing. I didn't want to choose. I wasn't about to proclaim my undying love for either of them…but that didn't mean I couldn't get to know them a little better, right? I wouldn't go so far as to say I was in love with either man, but you didn't have to be in love to have sex.

Jesus Christ on a bicycle. Look at me, flopping back and forth like a fish. Like picking off the petals on a flower: *to touch him, to not touch him, to kiss him, to not kiss him, to fuck him, to not fuck him.* I grew tired of the constant back and forth.

Fuck it. You only lived once, right? You only had one life, so you had to make the most out of every moment, and all that other Hallmark card bullshit, right? Plus, with how things were going around here, it'd be a miracle if I lasted the week.

We could brainstorm for a solution to the whole making-Bones-believe-us thing later. Right now, there was only one thing on my mind.

Maybe it was my expression. Maybe it was the fact that I was *this close* from being taken by a spirit. Or, hell, maybe it was just a long time coming, but Crane knew exactly what I wanted. He reached for me, pulling me in close with an abrupt intensity I didn't know he was capable of. His fingers splayed in my hair, holding my head steady, as if I'd try to pull away.

As fucking if. I was ready to go all the way with him earlier; he was the one who stopped us, not me.

His lips came down on mine, his neck bent to accommodate the height difference. His mouth was warm and heated, igniting a fiery passion deep within me. I didn't love this man, but I wanted him more than I ever wanted someone else. I wanted to rip off his clothes, run my hands all along his lean frame, and...

God, it was hard to think. So you know what? I was done thinking; here, tonight, I was simply going to do. No more internal debating, no more fickleness.

I set my hands on the collar of his shirt, tugging us both down to the carpeted floor. Crane rested on top of me, his mouth roaming along my jaw, trailing kisses up and down my neck, making me shiver over and over again. His legs pinned mine down, so long and lean compared to mine. Crane was a refined, hoity-toity kind of guy, but when the heat arrived, he could be just as sexy as the rest.

With the feeling of his lips on my neck, I worked at his shirt, practically tearing at the buttons, needing to touch his chest, feel his bare skin. Button by button I went, practically moaning when I felt him press his hips down on me, making me feel the hardness of his dick. We'd definitely crossed the path of no return now.

Once his shirt was completely unbuttoned, Crane practically threw it off. Before I knew it, we were both naked on the floor, our clothes in heaps beside us, our hands drifting along each other's body, taking in each and every curve, every muscle and tender place. His erection poked at me, but he didn't push inside. He'd taken off his glasses, so when his emerald eyes looked at me, I knew I was a bit fuzzy to him.

"I would prefer to take you upstairs, if that's alright," Crane murmured against my ear, an invitation I would never say no to. A man like him had to get down and dirty in a bed, but I didn't care. I didn't care where we did it, as long as we did it. As long as I finally scratched this everlasting horny itch I had.

I nodded, and Crane pulled me up. We left our clothes and his glasses on the floor as we headed to the stairs. Crane led the way, his hand holding mine with a firm grip. Step by step I followed him, thankful that Crane had enough money to have a big house with no neighbors close by—it meant no one could peer into the windows and see our nakedness.

Of course, as I made it to the top step, as Crane led me into his room, I started to wonder if I was spiraling. If this place, if Sleepy Hollow, was making me do things I wouldn't normally do. I mean, today I saw a murder. That didn't happen every day, you know? Kind of traumatizing. And to be a suspect in that murder...there was really nothing to compare it to. No other life experiences to use to make it not seem as terrifyingly momentous as it was.

I saw a man die—or at least I was in the same room as him when he died—and I was responding to it by having sex with one of the men who claimed to have feelings for me, even before he met me.

Nothing at all could go wrong here, right? This wasn't a recipe for disaster, was it?

It probably was, but oh well.

Crane pulled me close to him, our hot, naked bodies pressing against each other. His lips came down on mine, giving me a slow, tender kiss as his arms wrapped around me. Teeny step after teeny step, and soon we were on the bed, me underneath him, beneath the sheets. It was as if we never left, like we'd always been here, lost in each other, needing more.

Hands moved to my breasts, and I inhaled sharply as I turned away from his mouth, letting out a soft moan as he brushed his palms over my nipples. Sensitive things, they were. I ran my hands down his back, feeling his skin tensing under my touch.

Maybe I should've given him a warning: *having sex with you does not mean I'm yours, nor does it mean I'm in love with you. I'm simply using your body for your dick and nothing else.* Hmm…then again, maybe not. That might kill the mood a bit.

I spread my legs, the universal *welcome* gesture to a dick. Crane's mouth left my neck, and he propped himself up just a bit, his eyelids half-closed, his lips parted slightly. He took a moment to position himself, and even though he didn't have his glasses on, he must've wanted to watch me as he entered me. Our gazes locked, and it took everything in me to not close my eyes and look away when he pushed fully inside.

Crane let out a ragged breath once he was in, and then he leaned back down over me, his arms around my head, holding himself up as his hips began to set the pace of this fuck-fest. I kept my hands on his ass, liking the feeling of it as he pumped in and out. My back arched, and I finally let myself close my eyes, losing myself in the sensation of being taken, being fucked. There was always something so primal about it, something that made me even hornier.

A warmth spread in my lower gut, and I wanted more, more, more. It would never be enough, I felt like, when it came to Crane. This motherfucking town would be the death of me, but right now, I didn't care. Let Sleepy Hollow come for me. Let it take me. Let it do whatever the fuck it wanted to me. As long as I had Crane, I didn't care.

Whoa. That was…that was almost a thought of budding love, wasn't it? Shit. Better stop thinking and focus on his dick again.

I arched my back, and he pushed further inside, as deep as he could go without breaking me. The sounds of our sex filled the air, the twilight world outside inching towards total darkness. Sweat lined Crane's chest, his cheeks flushed. Every so often he let out a low moan, a sound I never would've pegged him capable of. Crane could be just as carnal as the rest, just as hungry, just as raw. It was good to know.

Crane's speed picked up the pace, and I cried out with the sudden roughness. His hips jerked, and he nearly collapsed on top of me, an earth-shattering moan erupting from his chest. He didn't pull out of me right away, he simply held himself there, his dick growing limp inside of me, his chest rapidly trying to catch his breath.

The poor man thought he was done? Hell no. He might've found his release, but I didn't have mine yet. This sexual encounter wasn't quite over just yet.

I pushed him off me, flipping us so instead he lay on his back and I straddled him. His dick hadn't slipped out of me completely, so it was easy for me to start riding him, and, big surprise, his dick got hard again. Which was good, because it was a lot easier to ride a hard one than a limp one. I mean, I didn't have much experience with the latter, but I could imagine how unfun it was.

I rocked back and forth on him, feeling his length slide in and out, dragging myself so far away that his tip nearly left me each time. I did what felt good to me, but Crane didn't seem to have any problems with it. His eyes were slits, watching me as I took charge, set the pace that felt good for me. His hands found their way to my hips, helping me rock back and forth but not changing my momentum. Crane let out a groan every now and then, and the sounds were like music to my ears. I liked hearing his groans; they were some of the hottest sounds I'd ever heard, probably because I wasn't expecting him to make them.

The pressure started to build inside me, and I let the pleasure take hold. An orgasm swept through me, causing me to throw my head back and cry out, heat flooding every part of my body, my toes curling. My inner walls clenched, and Crane sat up, moving his hands to my back but not flipping us to the way we were before. Since I was so caught up in my own orgasm high, he helped me move along him, his hips rocking beneath me.

Once the orgasm settled, I wrapped my arms around his neck, holding myself close to him as he thrust in and out of me. I could feel myself wet with both his cum and my own slickness, and I was more than content to let him come again. I'd been on birth control since I was eighteen years old; I wasn't worried about pregnancy, and from what it sounded like, Crane hadn't been with many other women, for he'd always longed for me.

Like a star-crossed lover or some sappy shit.

Crane's fingers tightened on my skin, his arms locking around me as his hips slammed up into me one final time. He moaned loudly when he came, squeezing his eyes shut and immediately resting his head on my shoulder, breathing hard.

We fell back to the bed, and he pulled out of me. I lay on my side next to him, and Crane kept an arm around me, still struggling to get his breathing back to normal. By the awe and the bliss in his expression, you'd think he just succeeded in doing the number one thing on his bucket list, or won the lottery, or something as impossible.

Maybe it was impossible. He'd worked with my dad, after all. All of the old stories, how Katrina Van Tassel chose Abraham over Ichabod, maybe Crane never thought he'd have me. He wouldn't have, if my dad wasn't dead. I never would've come back here. This town didn't call to me, or at the very least it never did before this.

Neither of us said anything for the longest time. Hell, I wasn't sure what to say. I felt like telling him that this didn't mean anything, that it was just sex and not a proclamation of feelings would've been too bitchy. Then again, I'd practically attacked him with a frying pan when I first met him, so it had to be a step up from that.

Crane let out a sigh. "I should get up, do some research. You should rest here, Kat. Take it easy. You've been through a lot today."

I wanted to smack his chest—which was a lot nicer than his slim frame would suggest. Crane wasn't overly muscled, but he hadn't an ounce of fat anywhere on him. He was lean, and a lot stronger than he looked.

Why was everyone's solution to trauma *resting*? Resting wouldn't do shit. I could help him research…even though I didn't know the first thing about researching things involving Sleepy Hollow. I had the feeling it involved more than Googling a few things.

So I resisted my urge to smack him, letting him get up. My eyes fell to his ass, watching as he went into the walk-in closet. "So the spirits have to know that I'm the key," I said, "to…whatever. Closing the veil. Opening it. Why would the Headless Horseman—" I paused, hating that I couldn't think of another word to say to describe what he did.

I wouldn't say he'd protected me, but no other words came to mind. Protecting me by killing someone. How twisted was that?

Crane came out, wearing pants but nothing on his torso. It was a good look for him, I'd admit. His brown hair was ruffled a bit from our excursions, and his eyes still had trouble focusing on me, but still, I was struck with the sudden thought of: *damn, he's cute.*

"I don't know if he wants the veil open," Crane spoke, sliding his arm into a shirt, one sleeve at a time. "I think his search for his head is his primary focus."

I bit my lower lip, wondering what the Headless Horseman would do if he found his head. Or, more likely, if I found it for him. Would he stop haunting the bridge? Would he kill me? Would he be able to cross over the veil like these other spirits and enact mayhem on Sleepy Hollow?

One thing was for certain. The Headless Horseman was the least of my problems now.

Chapter Thirteen

It turned out, doing research involved looking at a lot of old, musty books. Crane had a lot of them. After I showered and threw my clothes on, I did my best to help, even as the hours ticked into the night. Crane had a vague plan, but it was not one he would disclose to me, probably because I'd think he was ten different kinds of nuts. Or I would have, provided I never saw the Headless Horseman and was still in my own personal la-la land when it came to spirits.

All Crane kept saying was: "Your father and I were working on a few different things."

Okay, yeah. So specific.

So I kept my mouth shut, not knowing what the hell I was looking for. Basically, I turned into the food-fetcher. The drink-getter. The person who Crane told to fetch a pen and all the other useless stuff. Like I was some kind of assistant to his crazed brilliance. I wouldn't go so far as to label Crane or my father brilliant, but seeing as how this shit was real, neither were as crazy as I'd thought.

Sometime during the night, I must've fallen asleep in the chair near the windows in the library, because the next thing I knew, I woke up, the barest hints of sunlight streaming onto my face. As I came to, I found a blanket had been draped over me, laying atop my toes all the way to my hunched torso.

I sat up straight, a crick in my back from the uncomfortable position. Beneath the blanket, a book slid out, hitting the wooden floor with a thud. Stretching first, I bent to pick it up, snapping it shut as I glanced all around. The library was practically the size of my apartment back home, its walls full of floor-to-ceiling bookcases, jam-packed with ancient texts and leather-bound tomes. Some of it, I'd discovered last night, was in another language. Crane had told me he could read every single book in this space, which I just found ridiculous.

I sat in the only chair in the large room; Crane made himself at home at the desk. It was a wide, spacious thing, made of a dark wood, leather stitched into its top. Nearly a dozen books sat splayed atop it, most of them open to random pages—although Crane would never say they were random.

Crane, I noticed, was nowhere to be found.

I swear to God, if that bastard went to bed on a comfortable mattress and left me here only to get an ache in my lower back, I was going to kill him.

Tossing the blanket off me, I set the book down on the chair before marching out of the room, heading straight across the hall and to his bedroom…where Crane wasn't. The sheets didn't look touched since our prior intimate activities.

Huh.

I checked the bathroom; nothing in there, either. I headed down the stairs, checking the living room and the dining room, half expecting him to be there, sipping tea with a superior expression on his face. For him to look at me, smile, and proudly proclaim that he'd solved every single one of our problems. I fucking wish.

But nope. He wasn't there. He wasn't even in the kitchen, although I did spot something new hanging on the fridge. A note, like we were some couple in the fifties. A man and his housewife. I moved closer to the note, reading it over a few times before it actually dawned on me.

Went to the house, I will be back soon. Eat something. And then, because it was Crane, the note was signed with his real signature.

What a noob.

I reached around, feeling my pockets. Nothing but my cell phone. The bastard took my keys and went to my dad's house, all without waking me up. *How*? I would've felt his creeping fingers while I was sleeping in that chair upstairs, right? Crane wasn't that sly.

A gust of wind brushed past me, settling along my spine and causing the tiny hairs on my arms to stand straight up. An eerie calmness grew inside of me, and I immediately turned, finding that the set of glass doors that led to the patio in the back were wide open, the breeze gently blowing past them as if nothing at all was out of the ordinary.

But, you know, it was a little strange, because I knew for a fact those doors were closed a minute ago when I came out of the dining room. I knew, because wide open doors were something you tended to notice when spirits were after you.

I moved to the doors, glancing around as my hands found their handles. I was seconds from pulling them shut and locking them when a bead of sweat fell from my forehead, trailing along my nose, even though it wasn't warm. Even though I was in the real world still, I had the peculiar feeling that I wasn't alone.

I was being watched, but the question was, by who? What spirit lingered in the otherworld just outside these doors, wanting me to come out? Crane had said spirits prefer weak victims, so was the white-haired spirit just waiting for me to crack like an egg? Was that why the Headless Horseman was always nearby?

Fighting the unease settling in my gut, I shut the doors, flipping the lock just in case. Which was pointless, apparently, because locks and doors and windows didn't seem to be able to keep them out. Crane's house was warded, or spelled, or whatever the word was—protected by some of the best magical hoo-doo money could buy. My dad's house wasn't, because my dad had a thing for spirits.

I had no idea why. None of the spirits I'd met so far were very likable or friendly.

After taking a quick peek through the cabinets, I discovered that Crane had a lot of food stocked that I never tried before. Brands I'd never heard of, the kind of stuff you bought at those expensive, earthy grocery stores. I settled for coffee, heading to the grand couch in the living room once it was made and turning on the TV.

I flipped channels, curling my feet beneath my butt as I sipped my warm mug. Almost immediately, after five channel flips, I came upon a news station. They were, of course, talking about what happened yesterday.

Mike Reese, a local lawyer, found dead in his office. Foul play was obviously suspected, because how the hell could one inflict a wound like that on yourself, but the suspect pool was slim. I rolled my eyes when they started talking about how he was with a client when it happened, but it's unknown whether the client was the culprit, and I was seconds from changing the channel when the news lady came onto the screen, sitting at her desk with another man she was about to interview.

I didn't recognize the man, but something in the back of my mind told me not to flip channels, to hear what he had to say.

The newscaster was a pretty blonde woman, middle-aged but looking great. Then again, that could've been the makeup. Her bright blue eyes stared straight at the camera, almost like she stared right at me. "I'm here with Tom Wyland, a local historian of Tarry, and a firm believer in all of the legends of Sleepy Hollow."

Tom chuckled, running a hand over his green shirt. Couple that with his slightly darker green bow tie, his greying mop of hair, and the way his eyes darted back and forth, and he was exactly who I'd picture as a Sleepy Hollow historian. "All legends are rooted in some basis of fact," he told her.

The newscaster nodded, taking this whole interview way too seriously, in my opinion. Then again, a man was dead, so there was that. "You're here because you think there's more to the alleged murder of Mike Reese."

Tom leaned forward, laying his hands atop the desk, his fingers tapping the desktop. "There's always more to crime in Sleepy Hollow, Karen. If you take a look at the crime statistics, you'll find we have one of the lowest rates in the country—but for the crimes we do have, we have one of the highest rates of unsolved cases."

The newscaster, Karen, forced out a laugh so fake it jarred when it entered my ears. "I think that means Tarry needs a better police force—" Insulting the local cops? Not very nice, but I could tell Karen didn't believe half of the words this Tom said. She was only here with him now because the news execs forced her to be.

"No, it's because for most of these cases, the culprits aren't of this world," Tom cut in, dividing his time between staring at Karen and the camera. "It isn't a secret Sleepy Hollow is possessed. Everyone in that part of Tarry knows it. Windows open suddenly, car alarms go off in the middle of the night even though the vehicle wasn't tampered with…the list goes on. If you walk alone at night, you feel like you're being watched."

My breath caught in the back of my throat; it was as if I knew exactly what Tom was going to say before he said it: the bridge.

"There's an old bridge in Sleepy Hollow that's haunted. Everyone knows not to cross it at midnight. If you do—"

"If you do," Karen spoke, laughing, "you'll be haunted."

Tom was not amused. "Yes. It's the Headless Horseman's bridge." In the bottom corner of the screen, an image of a headless man shrouded in black appeared. It didn't look much like him, but it got the point across. "Some think the Headless Horseman isn't a real figure. The legend says Ichabod Crane was run out of town after riding home drunk. On that same bridge, he encountered a cloaked, headless figure, who threw his head at him. In the morning, there was no sign of Ichabod, only the battered remains of a pumpkin."

Karen was nodding again. "And people say it was the town hero, right?" She knew a little about the legends, but she wasn't a Sleepy Hollow resident. She wasn't knee-deep in superstitions.

"Yes, and Abraham Brunt went on to marry Katrina Tassel. They had a happy life, but not for long. Abraham was found dead in his bed a few months later, a deep gash in his gut."

I sat back, nearly spilling the coffee on myself. What was Tom saying? That Abraham pretended to be the Headless Horseman, and the original spirit himself didn't like it? Or...

"It was of course after Katrina was pregnant, which is why the town has some of his descendants today. But my point here is, even before that night with the pumpkin, there were rumors about that bridge and the Headless Horseman."

Karen leveled with him, raising an impeccably-plucked eyebrow as she asked, "Are you suggesting the Headless Horseman killed the victim yesterday?"

"I'm saying there have been half a dozen cases in the grove of Sleepy Hollow involving a similar death," Tom stated, pointing at the tabletop as if shoving his finger against it would make Karen believe him. It wouldn't. He sounded crazy, just like my dad, and as I watched the TV, I couldn't help but wonder if they'd ever met. If they were friends. He and my dad would've gotten along well. "In the last hundred years alone. That is not a coincidence."

Karen turned to look at the camera, saying something about a commercial break and they'd be right back. Then the news program cut out, leaving me to watch a commercial involving two older people, sitting in bathtubs as they held hands and watched the nature around them. Pretty sure it was a Viagra commercial.

I would've thought Tom as crazy as a crack addict before, but now? Now his argument made so much sense. Too much sense.

Ichabod Crane was drunk, sad that he wasn't winning Katrina's affections over Abraham, and he was so drunk he went to the one place he shouldn't have: the bridge that the Headless Horseman haunted. Abraham was waiting for him, dressed as the Headless Horseman, wanting to scare him out of town—and he did. But how long was Abraham there? Was he waiting for Ichabod when the clock turned midnight? Did he put a mark on his soul simply because he was playing dirty?

If Abraham was at the bridge at midnight, then the real Headless Horseman had marked him, followed him just like he was doing with me, only he didn't want Abraham's help to find his head.

The real story...it was more twisted than the legends said, and I didn't know what to do with that knowledge. I also didn't know where I fit into it. I was a spitting image of Katrina, and I felt drawn to both Crane and Bones in a way I'd never been drawn to anyone before. It was as if fate was laughing at us, telling us to replay history and reinvigorate the legend of Sleepy Hollow.

I didn't want to be Katrina Van Tassel, and I sure as shit didn't want Bones and Crane to replay their ancestors' roles. If fate wanted us to have a redo of the old legend, fate could go fuck off. I wasn't about to play. I'd shove that board far away from me so fast if you blinked, you'd miss it.

No thanks, I'd say. *Not happening. Not today, not tomorrow, not ever. I'm no rich damsel in distress, caught between two men. I'm...*

Well, I wasn't quite sure what I was, but I sure as shit wasn't rich.

I was in the kitchen making myself another cup of coffee when Crane returned, lugging in a black plastic bag that was labeled with two broomsticks crossed together. I turned to him, leaning my back on the counter as I brought the mug to my lips. "Did you have a nice stop at the witch store? Oh, and I believe you have something of mine."

Crane's green eyes flicked to me behind his glasses. He reached into his pocket, pulling out a set of keys. "Technically, they're you're father's keys—"

"Technically, they're mine now, since my dad is dead," I reminded him, a bit too snippy considering the subject matter of what we were talking about. I set the mug down, snatching the keys from him and stuffing them back where they belonged. With me, and not with him.

He got quiet for a moment, probably thinking about my dad, about all the stupid shit they'd get into together. Spooky research, scaring half the town with their the-veil-is-opening theories. Then again, after witnessing Mike being possessed, I didn't think they were such oddball theories anymore.

Unable to take the silence for long, I leaned on the island counter beside him, studying the black bag he brought in. "So what'd you get?" I asked, fighting the way my core warmed up in memory of what we did last night, how a secret—okay, maybe not-so-secret—part of me wanted to do it again.

No more banging Crane. That should go without saying, yet here I was, saying it. Or thinking it.

Whatever.

"And did you find whatever it was in the house?" I carried on, noting the way his eyes clouded over. A minute of silence passed, and I snapped my fingers before him, jerking him back to reality. "Earth to Crane. You in there, buddy?" Calling a man I just had sex with *buddy*? Yeah, I went there.

"I'm sorry," Crane muttered, pushing off the island and running a hand down his face. He lifted his glasses and pinched the rim of his nose. "I just...I don't understand it. When I reached your father's house, the front door was wide open. The whole house looks like a tornado went through it. Someone or something is looking for what I was looking for."

Somehow, the news of the house being tossed around didn't shock me. I guess Sleepy Hollow and its freaky, everyday happenstances grew more normal as the days wore on. My eyebrows came together. "How do you know what they're looking for?"

"Because it's the one thing not in the house," Crane said. "Your father's journal."

"Right," I deadpanned, suddenly remembering the journal was the be-all, end-all of this whole thing. "Because all of the secrets to Sleepy Hollow are in my dad's journal." Crane's look was all I needed to know that my would-be joke was more of a sad truth. "Tell me you're not serious. Tell me this is some elaborate joke that I—"

"It's not a joke, Kat," Crane said. "Every discovery, every spell and potion, each and every experiment we did that worked is in that journal. I have no way to replicate the potion without knowing the exact amount of each ingredient—I'd be doing guesswork—"

I blinked. "Spells. Spells and potions."

"Yes."

"Spells. We're really talking about spells here." Before Crane could respond, I let out a groan. "This is what my life has come to, huh?" I wanted to find a wall, label it with an X and bang my head on it, over and over. Then maybe I could forget about how weird this was.

"I'm afraid so," Crane spoke dryly. "However, the issue is not only with the potion itself. I remember most of the mixture, just not the specific amounts of each ingredient." He started to pull things out of the black bag.

I had no idea what they were, each ingredient was in its own tinier, see-through bag. One looked like dried leaves, the next appeared to be some white flower petals, and the last…well, the last bag looked like salt. Big, white chunks.

If I would've known we were getting our *Supernatural* on, I would've brought more badass outfits.

"I'll fiddle with it today, see if I can jog my memory." Crane let out a sigh, closing his eyes momentarily. "I was really hoping I'd find your father's journal."

"If the potion's not the main issue, what is?" Crane's jade eyes flicked to me, and suddenly I knew. "Getting Bones over here," I muttered, feeling my shoulders slump. After what happened, would he come if I called? I doubted he'd ever want to come to Crane's house, and convincing him to ingest a questionable substance was going to be difficult.

Crane held back a frown, although a slight downward quirk of his lips told me he was failing in holding it in. "Yes, Brom is the problem. Honestly, I'm not even sure this will work. It worked on your father, and it worked on me, but we never tested it out on anyone else before."

So Crane and my dad took field trips into the otherworld, huh? It didn't surprise me. What did surprise me was the fact that these two kept it to themselves. With how vocal my dad was about Sleepy Hollow and its legends, I figured he would have spread the word as fast as he could once he knew he had a something that could transport consciousness into another world.

I grabbed the nearest small baggie, the one with the white, salt-like chunks in it, running my finger along the plastic. "If Bones can keep the police off my back, you and I can try to figure out how to close the veil, or something." Yes, or something. Something to stop these spirits from coming after me for God knew what. Possession, something else, who knew? Either way, I didn't want to find out.

Crane nodded once. "You're right." His gaze rested on me, and I did my best to pretend I didn't notice it. He looked at me a bit differently now, as if seeing my orgasm face had brought us closer. It didn't.

What we did upstairs last night was just sex. Nothing more. No real feelings attached to our sweating, naked bodies. If Crane thought our sexcapades meant we were boyfriend and girlfriend, he had another thing coming.

But Crane didn't bring it up. He only got to work, pulling out a few bowls from one of the cabinets and telling me to fetch the measuring spoons in the silverware drawer.

Good. If he didn't bring it up, maybe we could pretend like it never happened.

Chapter Fourteen

A few hours later, I was sitting on the steps leading to Crane's giant front door, my cell phone in my hands. Luckily Crane had a charger for it, so I was able to juice it up a bit. I'd made the call I had to, got Bones to agree to pick me up.

How did I get him to come to Crane's house, his mortal enemy's lavish, expensive home? I told him that I'd made a mistake, that I missed Bones and needed to fully explain what had happened at Mike's office yesterday. Three things that I knew were sure to get him over here lickety-split.

Even after all this time, Bones wanted to protect me. He'd acted as my friend and my protector during our summers together, and that hadn't changed, even if he'd grown into a sexy beast of a man.

The breeze was soft and gentle, and I turned my face up to the sky. Crane had a few towering trees on his property, but none near the house, so I was able to gaze up at the clear blue expanse above me. Not a cloud in sight, which was odd for Sleepy Hollow. Its weather was typically one of dreary coziness, the kind of weather that made you want to grab a sweater and a book and sit near a window as the soft rain tapped on the glass. Spirits aside, this town wasn't a bad place to be.

The potion was complete, or at least Crane thought so. He'd done his best to replicate the potion him and my dad cooked up, but from what he said, the effects might be different. I had no idea what that meant, and I didn't particularly care. As long as it worked, as long as it got Bones back to my side, I'd be fine with it. Now the only thing left to do was wait for Bones to get off work and get here.

I heard the door behind me open, and Crane walked out, sitting his tall frame beside me. So far today, I hadn't seen hide nor hair or the Headless Horseman, or that freaky white-haired woman who was following me in the otherworld. It made me happy, but also filled me with a strange, inexplicable feeling of wistfulness, almost as if I wanted to see the Headless Horseman again.

Fucking stupid.

"I've thought about it," Crane said, and I glanced at him sharply, waiting for him to continue. I had no idea what the man was talking about. "It would be a terrible mistake to—"

To what? My mind went to the only place it could, since it was my mind, and last night was the first time in a while I'd orgasmed with the help of a dick and not batteries. It would be a terrible mistake to pretend last night didn't happen? A mistake to say we could never be more than friends? Was Crane trying to finally win Katrina and make his ancestor proud?

Of course, my mind completely jumped to the wrong conclusion. Go figure.

Here's the full bit of what he said: "It would be a terrible mistake to let you go with him. I'm going to drink it with him."

Ah, righty-o. The spell, the potion, whatever it was. Not our sex. *Because not everything was about sex, Kat. Get your mind out of the gutter.*

This potion thing would send their consciousness to the otherworld, or at least it was supposed to. Crane would drink it with him, and leave me with both his and Bones's motionless, seemingly lifeless bodies? No thanks. Talk about creepy.

"Why would you go with him?"

Crane spoke as if his answer should have been obvious, "Because the spirits are after you." Okay, yeah, he had a good point there. I, however, also had a good point.

"But the Headless Horseman will protect me. As long as he's around, the other spirits will stay away." Putting my faith into a murderous, headless man? Never thought I'd reach that point in my life. Welcome to the world. "Whereas if you and Bones go, who's to stop a spirit from getting to you guys?" I remembered what he said about spirits wanting to possess the easier, weaker people, but still. Being trapped in the otherworld? They'd look like two cool glasses of water to a bunch of dehydrated freaks who'd been stuck in the desert for years.

I mean, might as well make them a flashing neon sign, right?

Crane gave me an incredulous look behind his glasses. "You're saying you think you can stop the Headless Horseman from attacking Brom?"

"Uh, yeah, pretty much." I had more of an attitude than I wanted to have, and I tried to tone it back when I added, "The Headless Horseman wants me to help him find his head. I have no idea if I could, but—"

"But you'll use him to suit your needs," Crane finished for me.

"Well, when you say it like that, you make me sound kind of mean," I muttered, turning my gaze to the long driveway ahead of us. He was right, though. I wasn't above using the Headless Horseman for my own purposes—did that make me a horrible person? Did that mean I was going to Hell?

Fuck. Did I believe in Hell now? After everything that's happened in the last week, I just might.

"And if the Headless Horseman doesn't listen to you? If he still goes after Brom and you watch him cut Brom down?" Crane spoke, an unfamiliar wildness coating each word. "What then? What will you do when you come back to the real world and Brom is nothing but a vegetable?"

"That's what would happen if you die while in the otherworld?"

Crane whispered, "Yes. Your mind would be gone. Your soul. There would be nothing left other than your body." He reached for my hand, the one not holding onto my cell phone, no longer upset, but earnest. "I will not let you take that risk, Kat, regardless of how much you may care for Brom."

I was going to pull my hand out from underneath his, but when he spoke of Bones and my feelings for him, I froze. Crane didn't think we were together, even after last night. The Cranes lost when it came to Katrina Van Tassel, and I was her doppelganger. The man beside me probably viewed last night as some kind of consolation prize. I bet, in the end, he thought I'd choose Bones.

To that I could not say *fuck that* enough. Fuck it to fucking hell and back. This was the twenty-first century. I wasn't caught in some ancient love triangle where I was forced to choose in the end. This wasn't some teenage TV show where the female main character was caught between the friendly hero and the dark and mysterious new guy. This was my fucking life, and it was crazy.

It was so crazy that I had a ridiculous thought. It was a thought I'd had before, but this time I meant it very differently. This time, when I thought to myself *I won't choose*, I didn't mean it as if I refused to be caught in the middle. I meant it as I won't choose, as in I would stay in the middle for as long as the two men would have me in the middle. I could date them both. I could be with them both. They could each have me; everyone wins, right?

A pipe dream, I knew. Life wasn't so simple, wasn't so easy. Plus, dating them both would mean I'd have to stay in Sleepy Hollow, which a huge part of me still didn't want to do.

One thing at a time. I should focus on making Bones believe instead of getting ahead of myself.

I was about to say something along the lines of *you don't get to make my decisions for me*, but it was at that exact time a car pulled into the base of the driveway, its tires slowly rolling on the pavement as it came closer. I got to my feet, causing Crane's hand to fall off me as I headed for the car, which turned to park right in front of the house, the passenger side closest to me.

Bones sat in the driver's seat, his mouth a line as he gestured for me to get in.

Shit. This was going to be harder than I thought.

Instead of getting into the car, I headed around it, stopping only when I was able to lean down to the window beside him after sliding my phone into my pocket. Bones didn't look particularly happy, and I couldn't blame him. Things had been weird between us, ever since that night. It wasn't right. Being in Sleepy Hollow, I needed my friend back.

"What are you doing?" he asked, azure stare glancing at Crane near the house. Crane had stood the moment I did, though he did not step closer to the car.

"Bones," I said, gripping the car, "there's a lot we need to talk about. Please, come inside the house."

His muscular shoulders rose and fell once with a curt laugh. "I'm not stepping a foot inside that house," he muttered, his disdain for Crane evident.

I hated to do this, really I did, because it was such a bad use of the so-called feminine wiles, but I didn't see any other choice. I leaned down until my head was practically in the car, met his gaze, held it and whispered, "Please, Brom." I might've puckered my lips a bit and batted my eyelashes a few extra times.

I never used his name. Never. I thought it was weird to hear Crane say it. Speaking it just didn't feel right, but it did its job.

Bones stared at me for a while, a muscle in his square jaw tensing. A war raged behind his gaze, and I knew I was winning this. It was but a moment before he relented, sighing sharply as he reached for the keys in the ignition, turning the engine off as he said, "Fine. But only for five minutes."

"Thank you," I said, stepping away from the car and straightening my back as he got out. Together we walked to Crane, and I felt Bones stiffen beside me. He really didn't like Crane, did he?

No, I took that back. They didn't like each other. The animosity went both ways, and I couldn't help but wonder if it was this town, making us feel these things. Me and my weakness towards both Crane and Bones, why they were so drawn to me, and their hatred for one another. If so, Sleepy Hollow really didn't want us to be one big happy family.

The three of us went inside the house. Crane led us to the living room, but none of us sat down. Bones looked like he wanted to sprint out of the mansion as fast as he could. Crane's emerald eyes landed on me as he asked, "Would either of you like some—"

"No tea," I whispered, noting the way Bones frowned at Crane.

Crane and Bones couldn't stand to be in the same room as each other. How was I supposed to let them waltz into the otherworld together? I doubted they'd be holding hands and singing *kumbaya* while they were there. No, I had to go with Bones. I was the one Bones trusted here, not Crane. They'd merely be at each other's throats the whole time, too buried in their hatred to notice any creeping spirits.

It was settled.

At least, in my head it was settled.

"What's this about?" Bones asked me, acting like Crane wasn't in the room.

Crane didn't appreciate that one bit, for he started, "Perhaps I would be better suited to explain—"

Still staring at me, Bones said, "I didn't ask you, I asked Kat."

Hmm. Maybe being caught in the middle of them wouldn't be so fun after all.

"We have something to show you," I said. I hoped I didn't sound too particularly desperate, but these were bordering on desperate times. "Bones, I need you to trust me." Lightly touching his arm, feeling his warm muscles beneath my fingers, I whispered, "You do trust me, don't you?"

Bones wanted to ask what the hell I was talking about, I could tell by the way his lips thinned and his eyes narrowed on me, but he didn't. All he did was eventually say, "Yes."

"You're off for the night, right? This…it's going to take a bit longer than five minutes," I told him, my hand still on his arm. I didn't want to stop touching him. If anything, I wanted to touch him more.

I was suddenly reminded of that night in the cemetery, how hot and heavy we were getting. Me, pushed up against a tree. Bones, pressing his hard, wide body against me, his hands touching me in places I never dreamt of. Our hungry, desperate kisses…

Probably not the best thing to think of while both Bones and Crane watched me. I stopped that train of thought, but it was a little late. The area between my legs was already warm in anticipation. Damn it.

At least Bones was unaware of how turned on I was. It wasn't like I gave off a *fuck me now scent*, which was good. He studied me, asking, "What's going on?" Three simple words, and yet the answer to his question would not be as easy.

"There's something I want to show you," I said. "Proof." I finally tugged my hand off Bones's arm, giving Crane a nod. He went to fetch the concoction he'd been working on earlier.

When Crane was out of the room, Bones shook his head softly. "Proof?" he asked, sounding…sad? "If this is about what happened that night at the cemetery, I'm sorry. I overreacted. But, Kat, something is clearly wrong here. You were the last one seen going into Mike Reese's office. Unless you have proof that someone else was hiding in there, I don't see how—"

"Yes," I said, stopping him from saying anything else. Not exactly proof that someone else was hiding, but proof that someone else was there. Mike and I weren't alone. Telling him the whole possession thing would come later; the first step was getting him to believe I wasn't crazy, and neither was Crane.

Or, by extension, my dad. My dad wasn't crazy. Everything he raved about was true, and I never took his word for it. I'd hated his obsession with Sleepy Hollow and its myths because my mom blamed it as the reason for their divorce. I never once stopped to wonder what it would mean if everything my dad said was true, and now it was too late. He was gone.

He was gone, and I was spending the time I should've been arranging his funeral and selling his house to play with spirits.

"Yes?" Bones echoed as Crane slipped back into the room. "You have proof you weren't alone with him? Why didn't you say something at the station? Kat, you're the only lead right now, the only suspect." I didn't doubt if we were alone, he would've grabbed my hand and marched me back to the station.

Joke would've been on him, though. I had the feeling the *not alone* thing wouldn't be what he was imagining.

"That," Crane spoke, offering him a cup, "is where this comes in, I'm afraid." It was just a regular mug, nothing fancy. It wasn't like it screamed magic or anything. Just a normal, everyday, ceramic mug, and still it took Bones a minute to accept it.

Bones peered into it, his blonde brows coming together. "What is this?" His nose wrinkled, and he held in a gag.

Meanwhile I wanted to hold my nose. I refrained from it, but I did turn to Crane and ask, "Why does it smell so awful?" It was like someone had dug up a partially decomposed body and threw rotten eggs on it. Like if a sweaty armpit and a smelly fart had a baby, it would be this smell.

"Yes, I don't recall it stinking this badly, so I might've messed up the proportions a bit, but—" Crane's bumbling explanation was cut off when I grabbed the other cup from him. He was too caught off-guard to stop me.

"We have to drink this," I told Bones.

"No way in hell" was Bones's answer, which I was expecting, especially with the smell. Drinking it was the last thing I wanted to do too, but we didn't have any other choice.

"Kat," Crane warned, trying to grab it from me, but I kept sidestepping him. He might've been tall and lanky, but his reflexes were not as good as mine. I was able to dodge him easily, all the while keeping my gaze locked on Bones. "I have no idea if it'll affect you differently—"

There was only one way to find out.

"Please, Brom." Yes, I used his name again. Yes, I used it while coughing and wanting to vomit. "Trust me."

And then I downed the whole cup, gagging only once. Luckily it didn't taste as bad as it smelled. It was a thick, viscous liquid, a pale ivory color. A bit salty, too. It actually wasn't too bad, though the salted taste was a bit strong—

A world of black, of nothingness swallowed me up.

Chapter Fifteen

I woke up on the living room carpet, jerking to a sitting position as I glanced all around. Everything was as it was before, only the colors of objects were a bit off, a milky white haze over everything. A shroud over my eyes, alerting me to the fact that I was in the otherworld, that Crane's magical concoction had worked.

Only I was alone, no Bones in sight.

I swore to God I would strangle Bones if I wake up in the real world and find that he never even touched his own cup. I will wrap my hands around his neck, resist my urge to plant a few kisses on him, and strangle him. Hardcore strangle him. Because what the ever-loving fuck.

Getting to my feet, I glanced all around. The large house was even eerier when it was coated in an off-white color. I stumbled to the couch, planting myself on the nearest cushion. If Bones didn't come here, what would happen? I had a terrifying thought. What if he had a fit and took me to the hospital? What would happen to me if my body was moved while my consciousness was trapped here?

Shit. I wasn't sure, but I had the feeling it wasn't good.

I was seconds from reclining on the couch when I heard a manly grunt. Bones was on the floor before me, propping himself up on his elbows, having woken much less gracefully than me. His blonde head flicked all around, and his words said it all: "What the fuck?"

What the fuck indeed.

His blue gaze locked on me, and I crawled off the couch, moving to kneel before him. He looked aghast, a bit pale, but still just as sexy as he was in the real world. "Are you okay?" Wasn't sure why I asked. My first time here, I most definitely wasn't okay.

Then again, my first time here, I practically came face-to-chest with the Headless Horseman, so as first times go, his was coming along way better.

Bones said nothing as he got to his feet. I stood before him, watching as he took in his surroundings. "Where's Crane?" he asked.

"Crane's not here."

"What do you mean, Crane's not here? He was just here a moment ago." Recent memories flashed across his eyes, and Bones pointed at me. "You drank that stuff, then you collapsed. I was going to take you to the hospital, but Crane caught me by surprise and forced some of it down my throat. Next thing I know, I'm here." He ran both hands through his hair. "What the fuck?"

I waited a moment before saying, "If you've adjusted, there's more." If he didn't drink it all, he probably wouldn't be here for long. I had to show him everything I could before he faded away.

Bones gave me a look like *I* was the crazy one here. "What are you talking about?"

Lifting a hand toward him, I waited. Seconds ticked by, and his eyes fell to my extended arm. I had no idea whether or not he'd take it, but I'd drag him out of this house if I had to. Crane's home was warded against spirits, but the land wasn't. The Headless Horseman had to be somewhere nearby, and there wasn't any evidence that could beat a walking, menacing, headless guy.

With a slight frown, Bones took my hand, his warm, strong fingers curling around my palm. I led him out of the living room, into the hallway, and towards the front door. All the while he studied everything around us.

"Drugs," Bones muttered. "You made me high or something. Crane forced some kind of drug down my throat—"

I stopped with my other hand on the doorknob. "If this is all because of some drug, why would we have the same hallucination?"

He thought about it. "Okay, fine. You got me there, but still—this is too weird. This is—"

I shut him up by yanking the door open and pulling us both outside, onto the stone steps that led to the driveway. The sky above us wasn't blue; it was nothing but a thick, hazy white, like the world had been coated in a giant spiderweb. Everything's color was off. Some things were duller, but the grass was a vibrant green, almost blinding.

But Bones didn't notice any of it. He froze the instant he spotted the tall, headless figure looming straight down the driveway. The Headless Horseman sat on his horse, his demonic steed with glowing red eyes and steam coming out of its nose. His gloved fingers gripped the reins, and though he was far from us, I could see his impressive body tensing in preparation.

"Do you see that?" Bones asked, his voice trembling just a bit.

"I see him," I said. "It's not the first time I've seen him."

"That's the Headless Horseman," Bones muttered, turning his head toward me, but his eyes remained on the far-off figure. "Should we run?" He must've seen the headless man lean forward a bit and run a hand down his horse's neck, the way his hands gripped the reins with a new intensity.

He was going to charge us. Or at Bones.

Now was the time to put it to the test. It was quite literally now or never, and it could very well be the worst mistake of my life. Maybe even the last mistake. If my body became a vegetable…

No, best not to think of it like that. I would win this. I was right. The Headless Horseman would listen to me. At least I really, really hoped so.

"No," I stated, watching as the Headless Horseman grabbed the reins with a fiery passion, kicked his heels against the side of his steed, and took off, heading straight for us down the hazy driveway.

"Shit," Bones swore. He tried to grab my hand, to run back into the house, but I yanked my hand back, remaining rooted firmly in place. "Kat, he's coming—"

No shit, Sherlock, I wanted to say, but I found I could not say anything. I could only watch, fear rising in my gut, as the Headless Horseman and his horse galloped closer at full speed. The sound of hooves hitting pavement sent chills down my spine.

"Kat, this isn't a joke," Bones hissed, setting a hand on my shoulder, his fingers too firm around me to fight. He wasn't in uniform; he didn't have his gun. I doubted a gun would've worked in the otherworld, anyway. It was just us and the Horseman, and his horse—but who gave a shit about the horse when its rider was so damn impressive?

"No, but I have to know," I said, doing my best to fight him. I would not be dragged back into that house, not until I knew for a fact that the Horseman would listen to me. If he did…maybe we could use him against the spirits trying to break through the veil. Maybe there was another way to get rid of the spirits that broke through instead of killing the possessed host.

A woman could hope, right?

"Have to know what?" Bones was frantic, and I didn't blame him.

I wanted to turn and dart inside the house. Watching the Headless Horseman ride closer was not something

I enjoyed doing. The closer he became, the more I grew anxious. What if I was wrong? What if the Headless Horseman didn't listen to me after all? I put both my life and Bones's life in danger by trying this out.

It was too late now.

The Headless Horseman yanked on the reins, causing the horse to skid to a stop and rear. It stood on its hind legs for a few terrifying moments, the beast's bulbous black and red eyes on me as it kicked out its front legs and let out an ear-splitting whinny. Smoke seeped from its nostrils, but I stood my ground.

Bones, meanwhile, tried to play the hero and leaped in front of me, putting himself between us. Sweet, heroic, but totally misguided and misplaced.

The horse fell onto all fours, and the Headless Horseman slid off his steed, less than ten feet before us. Bones and I stood on the steps to the house, but Bones was two steps down. To get in front of him, I'd have to stand on the concrete, on the same level as the Horseman himself.

There wasn't a doubt in my mind that the Horseman would cut Bones down, so regardless of what happened next, I knew I had to be the one to face him, to tell him to slow his roll, to stop.

I had to tell the Headless Horseman to stop.

Everything that happened next happened in the span of five seconds, ten at the most.

I darted around Bones and situated myself between them, my feet flat on the concrete. The Headless Horseman moved closer, his hands curling, leather gloves clenching. His two-sided ax appeared in his right hand, and before he could raise it, before he could do anything more, I extended a hand, laying it flat against his chest—or his upper stomach, technically, since he was fucking taller than a tree.

The wind picked up, almost like a maelstrom of energy seeped from the Horseman, like he didn't want to be touched. He hadn't given me his permission, but I didn't care. I wouldn't let him hurt Bones, and if he was going to kill me, I'd go down swinging.

"No," I ordered, confident and firm in every way. I sounded like a queen, royalty who was used to commanding other people. Not to toot my own horn, but I sounded like a badass.

For a moment, it was just us. Me and the Horseman, two beings battling wills. Two beings fighting for control of this situation. No other spirits nearby, no other people. I even temporarily forgot Bones was behind me.

Neither of us moved for the longest while. I didn't know where to look. When one didn't have a head, where the fuck did you look? Definitely rude to gaze steadily anywhere below his waistline, but it just felt weird staring at his chest, at the black, ancient uniform clinging to his body.

My chest felt funny, almost like I could feel him staring at me—which was ten different kinds of stupid, considering he didn't have a head. "No," I said again, this time less confident, more unsure. I was unsure mostly because I couldn't get over how solid he felt beneath my hand. More muscular than Bones, definitely. Like a mountain shaped into a man.

Was it wrong to be sexually attracted to a body without a head?

"He's with me," I said, my voice nothing but a squeak. "You won't hurt him."

Behind me, Bones was busy muttering a string of colorful swearwords I didn't know he was capable of. The Horseman's ax faded away, and under my hand, his chest rose and fell with a single large breath.

Charged. My body felt charged, electricity zipping through my palm and up my arm. I was near motionless as the Horseman sluggishly reached for the hand on his lower chest, setting his own gloved one right on top.

Didn't try to move me, didn't pull away. Just stood there, with his hand above mine, as if he accepted it.

"Thank you," I whispered. The energy coursing around the Horseman had long since faded; the man was calm and I...I was so confused. Confused, bewildered, flabbergasted. All that good stuff.

What was going on here? This man, this spirit, was making me feel such strange, inexplicable things. Emotions I couldn't describe. I'd never felt like this before, had I? It was hard for me to say. *Hard*, just like the fucking chest I still touched.

"Kat," Bones broke into my confused reverie, drawing me back to reality. This wasn't a twisted love story between a girl and her headless boyfriend. This was a ghost story—er, a spirit story—and people were dead. Nobody else was going to die, not if I could help it, and if that involved using the Headless Horseman like a pawn in a chess game, so be it.

Sorry, buddy.

I slowly pulled my hand away from the Headless Horseman, feeling a strange coldness where I'd held my palm against him. Turning to Bones, I said, "Let's go inside. There's a lot we have to talk about."

Through the milky white haze of this otherworld, with the Headless Horseman looming behind me, what else could Bones say but "Okay"?

Bones was the first to head into the house, and I went to follow him, but I paused near the door, turning to look back at the Headless Horseman. He stood motionless at the base of the stairs, his wide frame heaving with a breath it was impossible for him to take. Hell, it should've been impossible for him to stand there, headless, but here we were.

A part of me felt guilty for leaving him out there, but it wasn't like I could invite him inside. I was ninety percent sure that even in the otherworld, Crane's house was off-limits to spirits. No, he'd have to stay out there. Plus, I had a feeling his presence would only further confuse Bones.

And me. It would confuse me too. It wasn't too long ago I was running from him, terrified that he'd use that ax to end my life. Things progressed rapidly in Sleepy Hollow.

I went inside the house, immediately stopping. The door swung shut inches behind me, and I stood staring at Bones, who gave me the strangest look he'd ever given me in his life. All those summers we'd spent together, all those carefree days when we had nothing but ice cream on our minds, and not once had he ever stared at me like I'd suddenly sprouted a second talking head, a head that just insulted both him and his mother.

"What?" I asked, feeling my heart speed up for a totally stupid reason. Like I was just caught by my boyfriend ogling another guy. Which A) Bones was so not my boyfriend, and B) the Headless Horseman was not boyfriend material. Even if he wasn't an ax-wielding spirit with a thing for murder, he's headless. Sorry, call me shallow, but I'd prefer it if my significant others had heads. Tongues were kind of necessary for, uh, certain things.

"*What*?" Bones echoed. He rose a hand, gesturing toward the door, toward outside, at the Headless Horseman. "What the hell do you mean, *what*? That was...I mean, am I going crazy? This is all real?"

"You're not going crazy," I told him. "This is all real. We're in the otherworld right now, which is why Crane's not here and the Headless Horseman is. Crane wanted to be the one to come with you, but I knew the Horseman would listen to me—"

"This is nuts," Bones whispered, his blue gaze heavy on me. It was clear he wasn't thrilled to find out this was, in fact, real and not made up. I knew the feeling; if I would've known as I was growing up that this shit was real, I wouldn't have believed my dad to be the town loony.

I slowly reached for his hand, entwining my fingers with his. Bones did not pull away. He only stared at me as I led us back into the living room and sat us on one of the couches, the one right in front of the giant window. The Headless Horseman stood outside; if he had a head, I'd say he was staring at us, but it was hard to tell, even harder to know what, if anything, he was able to see. I mean, his chest breathed and he knew where I was, so obviously he had to see somehow, right?

It was confusing, but also not the time to worry about it. It was time to explain everything to Bones— and I meant *everything*.

I started at the beginning, or at least the beginning of what I learned. I was sure there was still stuff I didn't know since I walked into this whole thing years late, but I did my best to relay everything Crane told me. How he and my dad worked together, how they were trying to do a bunch of different things, as crazy scientists often did, like close the veil and see the spirits in the otherworld, along with other things I couldn't remember. How Crane thought that maybe a spirit had hurt my dad, all to bring me here, because I was the fucking reincarnation of Katrina Van Tassel.

Anything and everything I could tell him, I did—and I did it fast, because I had no idea how much longer we had here together.

Bones took it like a champ, only giving me a stupid, open-mouthed look twice, and both those times were when I was explaining everything about the Headless Horseman, how he was following me, protecting me from other spirits…how he wanted me to help him find his head.

"You're saying that thing out there is who killed Mike Reese?" Bones asked, turning his head to glance outside. Our fingers were still intertwined; neither of us had pulled away once we sat down. It was easy to forget we were touching, almost like it was the most natural thing in the world, as if this was how things should be.

I nodded once. "But Mike was possessed—"

"So in a twisted, murderous way, he was saving you," Bones muttered, eventually drawing his blue gaze to me. He trusted me, but distrust for the Horseman lingered. "The spirits want you to…open the veil, which is what separates this place from the real world, and the Headless Horseman wants to protect you so you can help him find his head."

Yes, yes, he was getting it. Bones caught on faster than I did, when Crane was telling me all this stuff.

"You're not going to help him, are you?" Bones asked, his fingers tightening around mine. "He's a killer. If you help him, there's no telling what he'll do."

"He listened to me," I said, as if that explained it all. It didn't, and I knew there was no excuse for murder. Even if Mike was possessed, he was still a person. A living, breathing person that the Horseman had snuffed out.

Bones shook his head once. "And he'll probably stop listening to you once you help him. Kat." He paused, reaching for me with his other hand, swiping some of my auburn hair behind my ear, his fingertips lightly grazing my cheek, sending heat flooding through me. Our bodies slowly angled toward each other, and my lungs filled with a deep breath. I held it in as Bones continued, "I know you probably think you need him, but you don't. You have me, and Crane."

I held in a chuckle when he mentioned Crane. The blueness in his eyes darkened a bit; it was more than obvious to anyone who could read social cues that he only brought up Crane's name begrudgingly.

"Whatever this is, whatever's going on, we'll figure it out." The hand that had tucked some hair behind my ear fell to my shoulder, running down my arm. "I won't let anything hurt you. If a spirit wants to get to you, they'll have to go through me, first."

It was a chivalrous offer, but one I didn't want to take him up on. I knew Bones would gladly put himself in harm's way for me, but that didn't mean I wanted him to. No, I refused to let anyone else die in Sleepy Hollow because of me. This puzzle, this confusing thing, would not result in any more deaths, I would see to it.

"Bones," I whispered his name. It'd been his name since we were children, a stupid nickname at first because he hated his birthname. As a kid with the first name of Brom, I couldn't blame him. I'd hate that name, too. Bones was so much cooler, and even though I had a crush on him growing up, I never quite knew just how amazing this man was until now. Until I was forced to come back and realize that even though I hated Sleepy Hollow and its myths and legends, I was as connected to the town as anyone could possibly be.

I was Kat Aleson, but I was also Katrina Van Tassel. This was my story, my strange tale…and you know what? I was going to become the writer. This story would go how I wanted it to go—and right now there was nothing else on my mind but the man beside me and the feeling of his warm, strong hand entwined with mine.

"I won't let you die for me," I added, meeting his gaze, which suddenly seemed much closer than it had been a few moments ago. Was Bones leaning in, or was I? Didn't matter much either way, because with the rate my heart beat inside my chest, I knew I wasn't going to pull away. This, Bones, it'd all been such a long time coming, and I was tired of denying it.

Plus, he and I needed to continue what we were doing that night in the cemetery, right? This time the Headless Horseman wouldn't interrupt us. No stray spirits could break into the house we were in. It was just me and Bones.

Just as it should be, a part of me chimed in, but I fought that part from taking over. Doing anything with Bones right now didn't mean I was choosing him; it simply meant I wanted him. Honestly, what straight woman wouldn't? He was thick and muscular, yet his hands carried a gentleness you wouldn't expect. This wasn't because we were our namesakes.

What we were about to do had nothing to do with history.

We would make our own.

Chapter Sixteen

Our noses were the first thing to touch, then our foreheads, and lastly our lips. It was a slow kiss, at first. Tentative in ways it shouldn't be, probably because I was worried how much time Bones had left here, but then we threw our caution to the wind.

Then it was all hungry mouths, ravenous hands, needing to touch, needing to grasp each other, needing so much more. More, more, more. Never sated, never enough. When Bones's tongue found its way into my mouth, pleasure warmed my core. He leaned us down, laying us on the couch, my back on the cushions and him above me, his strong legs pinning mine down. Hah, as if I was going anywhere. As if anything could stop us this time.

His fingers tugged at my hair while I ran my hands down his sides, then up his abdomen, touching his muscles beneath his shirt. Bones moaned into my mouth, grinding his hips down on me, revealing the erection that had sprouted up in the last few moments. He wanted me just as badly as I wanted him, and the thought made me even hungrier.

Bones's lips left mine, my mouth feeling the loss immediately. I was already panting, my chest rising and falling with each ragged breath. Bones was in much the same condition, but he had enough mind to ask, "Can we—"

I knew what he was going to say, because it was more than obvious what was on his mind. It was on my mind, too. Can we have sex while our consciousness was in the otherworld? Who knew—but there was no harm in trying to find out, was there? Besides, it didn't seem like he was having issues getting it up, so I could only imagine how wet I was underneath the hood.

"I don't know," I said, "but I don't want to stop." My voice came out fluttery and light; I hardly sounded like myself.

Bones's wide chest let out a grumble of agreement, and before I knew it, he was working at my pants, undoing the button and the zipper before sliding a few fingers along my most private part to gauge my readiness. When he touched me there, I could feel the slickness. I was practically dripping wet; it would be impossible to be any readier than this.

His hand withdrew from me, and he tugged everything below the waist down on me, past my knees. After, he worked on himself, freeing his cock. Were we really about to have sex in the otherworld, with the Headless Horseman just outside?

Yes, yes we so fucking were.

When the tip of his cock pressed against my entrance, I bit my bottom lip, locking eyes with him. For some stupid reason, this momentous. The connection I had with him, my childhood crush, everything was at a peak now. Whatever would happen after this didn't matter. I wanted to live in the now. I wanted to feel that thick dick inside me, and I wanted to hear Bones's moans in my ear when he came.

Bones pushed his hips against me, driving himself deep into my core, lighting me up in ways I never knew possible. I felt full, as if my whole body could feel his dick. When he began to thrust, I inhaled, arching my back to allow him to drive into me deeper. As deep as he could go without breaking me.

Hell, even if he wanted to break me, I wouldn't mind. This was like heaven. Heaven on earth—er, heaven in the otherworld? Whatever.

Bones tried to kiss me as he thrust into me, but he was lost in his own pleasure. I didn't mind, because I was focusing on the feeling of his dick, too. Like it was made for me. My dick. Everything about him was mine. I claimed him. I wasn't going to share him. Call me selfish, but I wanted both Crane and Bones. This was the twenty-first century; a woman didn't have to pick, did she?

I mean…why choose?

The sounds of my wetness filled the air, mingling with Bones's grunting and my gasps as his thrusting grew harder. Our eyes locked, and I could see the hunger in his gaze, the way he wanted to eat me up, have me again and again and it would still never be enough. I hoped I gave off the same look, hoped he knew that I was a liar if I said this didn't mean anything.

Yes, I was a horny bitch, but I was only a horny bitch for him. And Crane, but Crane wasn't here. It was just me and Bones.

My fingers tangled in his blonde hair, tugging it gently, exposing his neck to me. I brought my lips to his neck, kissing him, sucking on him, feeling his shoulders start to shudder. He liked the neck kissing, apparently. I ran my tongue up to his jawline, and was just about to give him a deep, earth-shattering kiss when, just like that, he was gone.

Bones was gone, his dick too. I was suddenly alone on the couch with my aching vagina and my pants and panties tugged down to my ankles.

I threw my head back on the cushion, letting out an annoyed, frustrated sound. All I wanted to do was fuck Bones. Was that too much to ask? For the whole Sleepy Hollow thing, the whole doppelganger bit, it felt oddly impossible to do it, like every outside force wanted to give me lady blue balls.

Ugh.

Well, I was probably going to be stuck here for a while longer by myself, so I had time to take care of myself. My fingers were not as good as someone else's—or a mouth, or a dick, for that matter—but they would do just fine.

I brought a hand between my legs, feeling my own wetness. I brought some of it from my entrance up to my clit and started stroking away. My eyes closed, and I pictured Bones on top of me, pounding away with wild abandon, as if we'd never stopped. I imagined his moaning, the feeling of his wide, strong body above mine, how his dick filled me up perfectly, right to the brim of what I could handle.

My skin flushed, growing hot. My breathing grew rapid, and my hand's pace picked up. Toes clenching, I worked at the eager nub at my apex until I felt the pleasure building inside of me, until the ball of heat released and flooded every part of me, like electricity tingling my every muscle. I let out a cry when I came, wishing Bones was here to hear me.

Hands were fun, don't get me wrong, but the real thing was so much better.

Sighing to myself, I rested my arms above my head on the couch, laying there with my midsection exposed for a while. Had to give my body some time to calm down, didn't I? I smiled to myself as I wondered if Crane had seen an erection start to grow on Bones's unconscious body. That was a telltale sign if there ever was one. Kind of awkward, but also kind of hilarious.

At least my turned-on body was easy to hide, unless Crane was touching me while unconscious, which I didn't think he was. With how he acted, I was pretty sure the man grew awkward while even thinking of doing something inappropriate…until the clothes were off, then he became somewhat of an alpha.

I let out another explosive sigh as I sat up and tugged my pants and everything back up. I swung my legs off the couch, looking around. I supposed I could snoop, but my peripherals spotted the Horseman still standing outside, having not moved a single muscle in all that time. Well, other than his expansive chest that could hold the entire freaking continent of Russia.

I got to my feet, pausing when I still felt a little tingly between the legs, waiting for the feeling to pass before I headed back outside. The demonic horse stood ten feet away on the driveway, its hooves pawing at the ground. I ignored its red, fiery eyes as I moved before the Horseman, whose feet nearly touched the bottom step of the marble stairs.

His chest rose and fell steadily, breathing breaths he should have no right to take. The laws of nature must not affect him in the same way they affected everyone else. He was above them, in his own terrifying league.

And yet...here, now, I wasn't afraid. Maybe I'd grown bold since he listened to me, since he stopped from hurting Bones. Or, hell, maybe simply seeing him so often was making him less intimidating and frightening. Then again, perhaps I'd just become numb to it, to him. Sleepy Hollow was morphing me, twisting what I thought was right and wrong.

I stared at his chest as I spoke softly, "Thank you." I would never get used to not looking someone in the eyes when I was talking to them. When he said nothing—because what could he say without a head— I added, "For not hurting Bones. He means a lot to me."

Imagining Bones being hurt, cut down in front of me, made me instantly sad. "I don't know what I'd do if something happened to him."

The Headless Horseman's chest rose and fell with another breath, and I was once again struck by how impressive he was. Even without his head, even while I stood on the step before him, he was still taller than me. How tall would he be with his head? Six and a half feet? Taller? My head spun even though it shouldn't. I shouldn't care how tall he would be with his head. He was a murderous spirit who…who I should have no feelings for.

I opened my mouth to say something more, but the Horseman stunned me by sluggishly lifting a hand, bringing it to my face. He was going to touch me, brush his fingertips against my cheek, and yet he stopped himself short. One more inch was all he had to close, but instead he withdrew his outstretched hand, curling his leather-bound fingers into a fist as he let it drop to his side.

I very nearly told him he could touch me, but a strange, new feeling started to spiral around me, originating in my gut and slowly growing until it enveloped me completely. The otherworld grew even fuzzier around me, and soon the image of the Horseman standing in front of me faded away.

I woke up on the floor in Crane's living room, inhaling a giant breath as I looked all around. The colors were normal, the sky outside a crisp blue outside. No more otherworld; no more Horseman. And, wonderfully enough, no temporary blindness accompanied with tears of blood. I was a bit nauseous, but I'd take nausea over bloody tears any day.

Crane was kneeling by my side in an instant; Bones was nowhere in the room. I set a hand on my head, watching as Crane's green eyes studied me. "How are you feeling?" he asked. "You shouldn't have done that."

"I'm okay," I said, swallowing down my urge to vomit. "And it's a good thing I did do it, because the Horseman was there, and he nearly killed Bones." Crane helped me get to my feet. "Speaking of Bones, where is he?"

"Ah, yes," Crane's voice took on the typical uneasiness, "he said he felt like being sick, so I directed him to the bathroom." He said nothing else, even though I could tell there was something else on his mind.

I crossed my arms before my chest, demanding, "What?" I didn't like the look he had.

"While in the otherworld, did you and Brom—"

I let out a short laugh. "That, Crane, is none of your business."

And it wasn't. It wasn't as if I pledged myself to Crane and only Crane when we had sex. Nope. I was still a free woman, able to sleep with whoever I wanted whenever I wanted, whether I had a weird connection to him or not. I had the same connection with Bones, anyway. Me and connections in Sleepy Hollow were a dime a dozen, apparently.

It was but a few moments—and a whole pot of tea later—that Bones joined us in the living room, looking only a little pale. I didn't touch the tea before me, but Bones grabbed a glass, drinking the whole thing before he slammed it onto the coffee table, startling both Crane and me. "Now what?" he asked, looking between us.

Outside, the world descended into night. Crane had closed the curtains behind us, turned on the lamps on the end tables adorning the room. It created an eerie atmosphere, and yet I felt comfortable in it. Crane sat on a chair opposite me, while Bones refused to sit at all. I couldn't blame him for being freaked out. When I learned about this stuff, it wasn't pretty.

"Frankly, I don't know," Crane muttered, running a slim hand down his face. "The only thing I can think of to do is to try to create a warding charm to keep the spirits away from you," he told me. Glancing to Bones, he said, "But as for what we do about the veil, about the spirits going after Kat, I'm afraid I don't rightly know."

"The Horseman," I said, earning stares from the both of them. Neither man looked too happy with me bringing him up. "He has to be connected to this. I mean, he has to have been here the longest. He's haunted tons of people."

"And probably killed more than that," Bones muttered, a muscle in his jaw tensing.

Crane heaved a sigh. "As much as I am loath to agree with Brom, I think he's right. The Headless Horseman is a killer. There's no telling that he's connected to the spirits, or if you help him get his head, there's no telling that he'll simply vanish. He might decide to wreak havoc on the entire town instead of merely that bridge."

I knew where they were coming from, and I knew how crazy I sounded, but I just couldn't help the fact that I felt as if the Horseman was connected to all of this…connected to me. Was it only because I walked over the bridge at midnight, or was it some divine plan, like the whole Ichabod versus Abraham thing?

Never thought I'd be stuck in one of those cheesy star-crossed lovers books. Then again, until recently, I never thought spirits were real. Things changed fast, and I regretted spending my childhood thinking my dad was crazy. If my mom had known my dad wasn't nuts, would she have stayed with him? Would they still have gotten divorced? I didn't know, but it did make me wonder.

Still, I knew it was pointless to argue with Crane and Bones about the Horseman. There was no way they could understand how I felt about him, the bizarre mishmash of feelings inside me. It wasn't like I could make them feel what I did.

"She was able to stop him, though," Bones told Crane, sounding, surprisingly, amicable. "He was intent on killing me, but when she told him to stop, he did." It took him a while to add, "He might want to hurt others, but I don't think he'll hurt Kat."

"The spirits know who's close to her," Crane said, rubbing his chin. "They'll try to go after anyone they think is a link to her, including you or I, if they can get their claws into us, weaken us until we're easy to possess."

Bones stared at him for a long minute. "Great. Spirits trying to possess me. Can't wait for that."

"They'll go for the easier targets first, but…" Crane glanced at me. "I don't know who else you know here in Sleepy Hollow, so I have no ideas on who they'll seek to go after next. We have a few days before the same spirit that possessed your father's lawyer returns, but there's no telling how many other spirits have crossed over and are waiting for their time to strike."

Right, so basically I was never safe, no matter where I was, unless I was in this house. Who the hell knew how many spirit eyes were on me, peering through windows and peeping through door cracks. If I left this house, I wouldn't be safe. It was only a matter of time before one of them snatched me and…did whatever it wanted with me.

Bones frowned to himself, crossing his arms, his muscles bulging with the movement.

Crane took another sip of his tea, reclining in his chair. "I don't know what their endgame is, but we can only assume it has something to do with opening the veil completely, which, I shouldn't have to explain, is a very terrible thing. Imagine countless amounts of spirits, roaming the streets of Sleepy Hollow at all hours, every day. So many spirits that they break through the confines of city limits and start to take over the entire state."

I knew where he was going with this. State by state until the whole country was overrun by spirits. Then the continent, then the hemisphere, and lastly the whole world. The veil could not afford to be broken.

"And," Crane added, "usually rituals revolving around something so large as shattering the veil between the earth and the otherworld involve a sacrifice. Blood, or life." To me, he said, "I wouldn't doubt that the spirits would kill you, if they knew doing so would open the veil."

Oh, great. So I only stared my death in the face? No biggie. No problem at all. I could totally handle it; I mean, I'd handled problems like that before, right?

No, no I haven't. I'd never faced anything so important before, but I knew the one flaw in Crane's plan. The spirits might kill me, if they knew it would open the veil. The spirits might try to kill me...unless another spirit got to me first and possessed me. The white-haired spirit from the otherworld came to mind. She wanted me, and she was only kept at such a distance because of the Headless Horseman.

Holy shit. This was one confusing mess. I needed a nap. Or, you know, a full eight hours.

"Well," Bones started, glancing at me, "just keep me in the loop. Now that I know, I..." He shook his head. "I don't want to be blindsided by any of this again." He noted the darkness outside, past the curtains. "It's getting late. I should go. I have work tomorrow, unlike some rich kids." Back to throwing barbs at Crane.

Before Crane could say anything in response, I got up, moving toward him. "Let me walk you out," I offered, to which Bones simply nodded.

I went with Bones to the giant front door, stepping outside with him but not going down the steps. The night air brushed against my skin, cooling me down. Truth be told, I was still a little hot and bothered from our earlier encounter in the otherworld, and as I stood there beside him, I couldn't help but wonder why we were always interrupted.

I opened my mouth to say something, anything, but Bones beat me to it. He stepped closer to me, digging his hands in his pockets as he said, "About what I did before, what I said…I'm sorry. I had no idea any of this was real. If I would've known—"

I blinked. He was apologizing for freaking out at me earlier? I mean, yeah, I'd been kind of pissed at him after the cemetery incident, but I didn't think it needed an apology. "It's okay."

"No," he said. "It's not okay. I shouldn't have stormed off like that, left you to fend for yourself with Crane. I feel like the world's biggest asshole."

"You're not."

"I feel like one—"

I leaned toward him, running a hand down his arm, stopping him from saying anything else. "You're not," I whispered, hoping he believed me. I didn't need Bones, the freaking town hero, to think he was a bad guy. Everyone had their good and bad moments. I didn't hate him for freaking the flip out when I'd brought up the Headless Horseman after going blind and crying a few bloody tears. He had every right to freak out. "You, Bones, are one of the best guys I know."

Dimples appeared on his cheeks, and a slow smile spread on his lips. Lips looking so very kissable right now, but I held back, not wanting Crane to see. "You keep flattering me like that, and my ego just might get as big as Crane's."

A laugh escaped me before I could stifle it. "Crane's ego is not that big," I said. A man with a huge ego wouldn't have acted so embarrassed after I'd come onto him that morning.

Bones stared at me like I was stupid. "Kat, you have to see it."

"See what?"

"The way he acts around you is…" He shrugged. "Just different than how he acts around everyone else. He's putting on a show for you. He wants you to like him."

"Are you saying Irving Crane is fluffing up to impress me?"

"I'm saying he's trying to. Whether he's actually doing any impressing, that's on you."

I gave him a coy smile. "Stop worrying about Crane. Worry about the spirits instead. Actually, worry about anything else besides Crane. Let me handle him." Crane might be putting on airs around me, but in a way, I found it kind of sweet. No guy had ever tried to impress me before, or maybe I just never noticed. As long as Crane wasn't an ass deep down, I didn't care what he acted like.

"Fine," Bones said. He leaned his head down, but he didn't close the distance between us entirely. I could feel his hot breath on my face, and I warmed in other, lower places, wishing our time hadn't been cut short. "But know that sooner or later, I'm going to have you all to myself, because I'm tired of the interruptions."

His forwardness stunned me into silence, and he responded by smirking, placing a gentle kiss on my forehead, and leaving. I watched as he strolled to his car, dumbfounded and more than a little turned on.

Damn it, Bones. Now I have to go inside and pretend to not be a horny little freak. Thanks a lot.

When I returned to Crane, I found him gingerly sipping his tea. The expression his regal face wore was not one of friendliness, although when he spotted me, the hard expression softened. "Ah, you're back. I was just starting to think that you'd decided to go off with him—"

I resisted my urge to glare at him. I did, however, say, "Whatever rivalry you and Bones have going on? It needs to stop. I don't want to hear it. You don't like him, he doesn't like you. Blah, blah, blah. I get it. You've killed the horse and are now beating it over and over again."

"I don't think we've gone that far," Crane said dryly.

"I do, so stop. Please."

Crane let out a sigh. "For you, I suppose I can hold my disdain for Brom inside."

Honestly, after I'd slept with him, it was the absolute least Crane could do.

Chapter Seventeen

The days wore on. Bones swung by Crane's house any chance he got, on his lunch breaks, after work, on his days off, all to see where we were at and give us updates on the investigation into Mike's death. Though I was the only suspect, they had no other leads, no evidence linking me to the murder weapon or anything. Bones was doing his best to help the department steer clear of me, but I knew it would take time. Mike's case was one that would remain forever open, I would say.

Crane and I spent our time researching. I never left his house, because he swore to me he was having some kind of moveable ward created for me—again, the best money could buy, whatever that meant. He ordered some clothes for me online, too. I personally thought it would've just been easier to make a short trip to my dad's house, but then again, it wasn't like Crane didn't have money to spare.

It was one particular afternoon when we were in the kitchen, taking a break to eat, when I asked him, "Why can't you do the wards yourself?" I had an empty plate before me, having devoured the sandwich Crane made me.

Yes, I made him cook for me. The man bent over backward for me anytime I wanted, so what was I supposed to do? Cook for myself? Fuck that. Food always tasted better when someone else made it for you. Fact.

"Your father and I discovered that we were able to do many things," Crane started, his eyes glancing at me from behind their glasses. Today he wore a striped polo, cleanly pressed pants as was his usual style. Dorky, but still somehow attractive to me. The complete opposite of Bones. "There are, however, some things that remain solely in the hands of women."

I gave him a *come on* look. "Sexist, much?"

"I didn't mean it like that," Crane quickly said, his cheeks turning pink. It was adorable. I loved it when his pale cheeks flared up in embarrassment—it was also surprisingly easy to do, considering we'd had sex before. I mean, there should be no more embarrassment between us, right? "I simply meant that, as a whole, women are more attuned to nature…usually."

If he wasn't careful how he progressed from here, he might get a slap on the face.

"Witches," Crane spoke, noting the annoyance on my face. "I'm talking about witches, not anything against women, or whatever it is you're fuming about. Men simply cannot be witches."

"But you can be wizards," I muttered.

"This isn't *Harry Potter*. Men have some power, but nowhere near the level witches do if they've been trained from birth."

Hey—I was a woman, and since I was a woman, I had a brilliant idea. "Why don't I make the wards?"

Crane gave me an unimpressed glance, though his gaze lingered on me longer than it should. "Have you been trained from birth in witchcraft? Do you have your own book of shadows? No? How about this: would you trust the wards you haphazardly create?"

Hmm. Okay, he had a point there.

"Fine," I mumbled, pushing the empty plate away from me. "But I am going stir crazy in this house."

"The spirits are staying away from you though, correct?"

"Yes."

"Then suck it up."

Crane's retort made me laugh. The way he spoke, telling me to *suck it up* was not something I ever thought I'd hear from him. The bastard. I was long past the point of caring for him more than I should; same with Bones.

And the Headless fucking Horseman? Yeah, let's not even go there. The headless guy was in my dreams more often than he wasn't, which was just weird. No more battlefields with dead bodies though, so I guess that was a plus.

After Crane cleaned up the plates, we returned to his massive library room. I asked him, "What's a book of shadows?"

"It can be a book, or even a journal that's passed down from witch to witch. They typically contain every spell a witch's ancestors could cast, and maybe even a few they never could. From my readings, I've ascertained that spells are fickle. They might come to you, but you might not have enough power to cast them," Crane rattled off, a bucket of useless information.

Who needed a TV when you had him?

Stupid. You always needed a TV, or at least I did. I loved TV. Couldn't get enough of it. In fact, if I was at home, if I wasn't stuck at work, I'd be watching TV right now. TV was mindless entertainment, and I loved it. I had the feeling I'd love it even more after I figured out the mystery surrounding this cursed Hollow. The things I enjoyed back then would mean more to me after dealing with all this shit.

"How do you know so much?" I mumbled.

"Kat, my dear, I've spent almost the entirety of my thirty years learning everything I could, especially about this place. Sleepy Hollow is…unlike any other place I've been to, and I've been to a lot. My parents liked to travel—they never felt as connected to this town as I do. It's why they live in Florida now, and not here."

My gaze fell, and I stared at my own two feet. "Do you think, since things are different here, we're all actors in a play? Like we're meant to have a redo of what happened before."

Crane watched me, his mouth thinning. "Do you mean what happened between the original Katrina and her two suitors?" After I nodded once, he eventually added, "I don't know. I guess that depends on you, because it's more than obvious Brom and I are following in the footsteps of our namesakes."

How could I tell him that I didn't want to choose? That being caught in the middle was the most unfair thing ever—along with being a target of otherworldly spirits? How could I tell him that, yes, I felt for him too, but I also had equal feelings for Bones? What sane man would want to hear the woman he liked say something like that?

I opened my mouth, about to say something, change the subject, do anything that didn't involve talking about the feelings I had for him and Bones, but my phone rang. It was currently plugged into an outlet in the wall, so I grabbed it, not recognizing the number. I picked it up, a pit settling in my lower stomach as I said, "Hello?"

Normally I never answered my phone when an unrecognized number rang. Ninety-nine percent of the time, it was simply spam. Someone from another country, telling me I won a cruise or asking about insurance for my new car, and then of course phishing for credit information and social security numbers. Older people might fall for it, but come on.

"Yes, am I speaking to Ms. Katrina Aleson?" It was a male's voice, and he sounded…unsure.

"This is she," I said, meeting eyes with Crane. "Who is this?" Something told me this wasn't a normal spam call. This, I had the feeling, was so much worse—and of course it was. This was Sleepy Hollow. Go big or go home.

"I'm calling from Memorial Hospital—"

Memorial Hospital was where they were keeping my dad's body until everything was figured out. Did they only keep bodies for so long? These were questions I never had to ask myself before. I should've looked it up, made a time frame for myself...I never thought my stay here would get extended on such extraordinary circumstances.

"—and it seems..." The man trailed off, sounding quite flabbergasted, considering he was the one who called me and not the other way around. "It seems we've misplaced your father. We've gone through security tapes, questioned everyone who's been to the morgue—it's like he vanished."

They couldn't find my dad's body? How? It wasn't like he could just get up and walk away...

I wanted to be sick. It took everything in me to say calmly, "If you find him, please let me know." And then I hung up, glancing to Crane, who watched the entire phone call in an elegant silence only he was capable of.

"What happened?" he asked.

"My dad's body…" The words felt strange. "It's gone. They can't find it at the hospital." I had a horrible thought, one that made me want to wish none of this was real. True nightmare fodder. "Can a spirit possess a dead body?" Just from the look on Crane's face, I knew I wasn't going to like his answer.

"Theoretically, yes," Crane said, pushing his glasses further up his nose, lost in thought. "But I have never heard of one doing it. Possessing a corpse would only be a temporary solution. The body wouldn't last long, not at all comparable to how long a living, breathing host would last. I mean, technically a spirit could possess a human for their entire lives."

"If it's the same spirit that possessed Mike…" I couldn't say more, and a chill swept over me, causing me to grow immeasurably cold. I wrapped my arms around myself, running my palms over my arms, trying to warm myself up.

Crane moved toward me, reaching for me, and before either of us could think better of it, he pulled me into a hug. He rested his chin on the top of my head as he said, "As long as you remain here, you're safe. No spirit can reach you in this house."

I closed my eyes, willing myself to believe him. Somehow, though, I knew things wouldn't be so simple. If a spirit had possessed my dad's body, where else could it go but here?

That night, as I lay down to sleep, I couldn't help but stare out of the window, at the full moon in the sky. Nearly full, I should say. Crane had a calendar in the kitchen, and I'd spent enough time staring at it while eating to know the full moon was tomorrow. The ward that I'd be able to wear around town should arrive within a few days, but still, I didn't feel safe.

How could I, when I knew my dad's body was out there, rambling around? And I knew it was; the hospital didn't misplace my dad's body. It simply got up and walked away.

I closed my eyes, pulling the covers over my head. I didn't want to think about it, but it was all my mind could picture: my dad's decaying body, rambling like a zombie, coming for me because the spirit haunting him needed me, or my blood, or my death, whatever. Though it was the absolute last thing I wanted to do, I felt the emotions welling inside, and my eyes teared up in spite of myself.

I cried myself to sleep that night. I cried even after I opened my eyes and found myself in a field, in dreamland, wearing an old-fashioned white dress. My fingers ran over the stitched fabric, and I went to wipe my cheeks. The same field, although this time there were no bodies. No battlefield full of rotting corpses and bloodied uniforms. The sun was hot overhead, and I sat there, hunched over, hating how messed up this was.

I didn't ask for any of this. I was fine with my normal life. I was fine with my low-paying job that barely got me by and dating guys for a month or two until I grew tired of them. I was fine with everything. This? This was some kind of medieval torture. This was downright awful, and I wouldn't wish this upon my worst enemy.

I stared at my lap for a while, at least until a large shadow blocked out the sun.

Right. Because I was never alone, not even in my dreams. I was connected to the headless man before me somehow, someway, just as I was connected to Bones and Crane.

I tilted my head up, meeting the tall, headless stature of the man in black before me. No ax, no demonic horse. Just him, looming over me like a giant. Like a thick, intimidating, headless giant.

"I'm tired," I whispered, feeling the weight in my bones. Sleepy Hollow was sucking the life out of me bit by bit, and it wouldn't stop until I was dead. That's what this whole thing was about, right? Me, dying to open the veil completely, letting all the spirits of the otherworld onto earth to wreak whatever havoc they could.

My blood. My death. Not to sound narcissistic, but this was all about me. The more I found out, the more I firmly believed my father was murdered in order to bring me here. Everything was carefully orchestrated, all for me.

"Is it because I look like her?" I asked a man who could never answer me, a man who could not speak. "Is it because I'm the spitting fucking image of Katrina Van Tassel? I didn't ask to be her doppelganger. I didn't ask for any of this." The more I spoke, the more enraged I became, until I could barely see straight. Until fresh tears coursed down my cheeks.

The Horseman was sluggish in kneeling beside me, his tall frame taking its time in bending toward me. One arm hung to his side, but the other rested along his knee, his fingers clenched in his leather gloves.

I didn't know why I said what I said next, but I did. Maybe because I was feeling shitty; maybe because I just needed to say it. "You can touch me," I whispered, glancing at him through watery eyes.

Telling the Headless Horseman he could touch me? Never something I thought I'd say.

There were a lot of things I never thought I'd say, but Sleepy Hollow was pulling them from me one by one at a record-setting pace.

The Horseman lifted the arm resting on his knee, uncurling his fingers as he tentatively brought them to my face. I closed my eyes the moment I felt the old, worn leather touch my skin, my breath hitching as his thumb ran across my cheek, his glove catching the water there and wiping it aside.

It's funny. With my eyes closed, I could imagine he was a person, that he had a head. That he wasn't a murdering spirit that had haunted Sleepy Hollow for centuries. He was just a man, and I was just a woman, caught in a bad situation.

I was measured in opening my eyes, staring straight at the place where his head would be. "If I live through this," I told him, his hand still gingerly touching my cheek, "I'll help you find your head, but no more hurting anyone. No more killing. That's the deal."

Crane would kill me if he knew I was telling the Horseman I'd help find his head. He would kill me if this town and its spirits didn't. Couldn't trust the Horseman, and yet I couldn't help but feel as if I could, even if he could go on a rampage. Even if he was a killer. Honestly, I shouldn't even think of helping him.

But I was. I *wanted* to.

The hand caressing my cheek returned to his side, and I hated to say it, but I felt its loss. He was gentler than his wild, ax-wielding side would reveal. His fingers curled into a fist, and he laid that same arm across his chest, his fist wound tightly against his upper pectoral. The Headless Horseman was kneeling, with a hand over his heart, pledging to me that he would heed my words and listen to them.

No more killing. Could the Horseman do it? I guess we'd find out, assuming I survived.

No more tears fell, and I felt my lips curling into a smile. I shouldn't be smiling; I shouldn't be excited for this, but deep down, a part of me was. "Okay," I said. "It's a deal."

Step one: survive the spirits trying to use me to open the veil to the otherworld.

Step two: deal with my dad's things and his funeral, assuming his body is found and it isn't overrun by some spirit.

And, last but not least, step three: help the Headless Horseman find his head.

Chapter Eighteen

I woke up the next morning invigorated, ready to take on the day. I flew out of the bed, about to find Crane, but something stopped me, causing me to freeze as I put on my ankle-high boots. The window to the bedroom was open, the cool, crisp air outside wafting in, an unwelcome and unwanted breeze.

After glancing all around and finding nothing else out of place, I went to close the window, wondering why these things kept happening. Did windows and doors just open by themselves in Sleepy Hollow? Didn't the wards on Crane's house stop spirits from coming in? I was confused; I'd have to ask him about it.

Once the window was firmly shut and locked—although neither of which seemed to matter much around here—I spun to leave the bedroom, but something new caught my eye, something dark and brown, resting on top of the bed I'd just gotten out of.

And the sheets…they were made. Expertly made, not a single crease anywhere that I could see.

Okay, something was definitely going on here.

"Crane," I called for him loudly, stepping toward the thing on the bed. The closer I got to it, the more I felt drawn to it. "Crane, come here!"

The thing resting on the bed was…a book. An old book, judging from its worn edges and spine. It was leather-bound, stitched with thick black material, at least three or four inches wide. A book like that had to be heavy; I certainly would've noticed it when I got up.

"Crane," I yelled for him again, as loudly as I could, now standing directly before the book. I loved books, but this particular one…an ominous aura radiated from it. I blinked, and suddenly the book came to life, opening of its own accord, its yellowed pages flipping by itself, stopping as it came upon a page with some words and a drawing.

The words were in English, but it was an old kind of English. I could read it, but it was difficult; some of the words weren't spelled right. The drawing was one of three circles, a pattern whose overlapped area was colored black.

The more I stared at it, the surer I was. Somehow, deep down, I knew what it was. Instinctual, almost.

A locator spell.

This was a book of shadows, but it wasn't mine.

I heard Crane's voice in the hallway, "I'm coming, I'm coming. Sorry, I was in the shower." Crane opened the door, stepping into the room, wearing nothing but a towel around his waist. A white towel that actually made his skin look somewhat tan. A towel that clearly hadn't dried him off yet, for the rest of him sparkled with water droplets. His brown hair, his gaunt jaw, his flat chest and abdomen… "What is it?"

He stared at me, not at the book on the bed.

I averted my eyes from his lower stomach, pointing to the bed. "That." Jeez, Crane was oblivious. Possibly the most oblivious person I'd ever met, which had to say something.

Crane blinked behind his glasses, which were a bit steamy. "What?"

"What?" I echoed, pointing harder. "The book! Don't you…" I stopped the moment I turned to glance at the book. Well, no fucking wonder Crane was looking at me like I was crazy. The book of shadows wasn't there anymore, and neither was its spell. It was just gone, like it was never there to begin with. My mouth dropped, and I fumbled, trying to find the right words to say.

Crane shook his head, moving to the window, closing it and latching it…which I knew for a fact I just did a minute ago. "You shouldn't leave the windows open, Kat."

I met his stare. "Spirits?"

Once again, he looked at me strangely. "Bugs," he said, as if it was the most obvious answer in the world. Crane left the room, returning to the bathroom, and I trailed after him like a confused puppy.

"Crane," I said, leaning on the door frame, not allowing him to shut it. The bathroom was steamy; the man liked hot showers. Right now, I was too freaked out to ogle his mostly naked form. "I shut that window right before I started calling for you."

His brown eyebrows came together. "But it was open when I walked in."

"Yeah, and there was also a book on the bed."

"A book?"

"A book," I said. "And not just any book, but a book of shadows. A book of spells. Crane, the book opened to a locator spell."

His emerald eyes studied me. "How do you…"

"I just know," I said, unable to explain how I knew. I just did. Simple as that. Why was Crane trying to make this so damn difficult? I wanted to take him by the lean shoulders and shake him…and then, maybe, do a few other things with him, too.

"Kat," Crane spoke slowly, taking a step closer to me. His eyes fell to my feet, slowly traveling up as he said, "If a book of spells appeared to you, that means someone wanted you to see it. And a locator spell…"

I came to the same realization he did. "Someone wants me to find the Horseman's head." Not just the Horseman; there was someone else out there who wanted me to help…but why? And who…

So many questions. Would we ever get answers?

"But if they have the book with the spell, why can't they just do it?" I asked, realizing how close Crane was. Two feet in front of me, still wearing nothing but a towel. Still wet. Still drool-worthy in his own, uptight way.

"Remember what I said?" Crane spoke, his voice a bare whisper. "Not every witch is capable of doing every spell."

"And spirits and spells—"

"Don't mix. Someone in town is a witch, and I bet they believe you're one, too. But why would they want you to find the Horseman's head? There has to be more to it."

I resisted my urge to touch him, to drag a hand down his chest and catch all the water droplets on its way down. "I'm not a witch though, right?" Me being a witch—it was crazy, wasn't it?

"You can peek into the otherworld without any help. There might be some side effects after, but I've never seen anyone do what you do, Kat," Crane whispered. He took a tendril of my auburn hair between his fingers. "You just might be."

If I was, I was untrained, new to all of this. Why would any witch think that I had the power to find the Horseman's head? Why me? Why any of this? Hell, why couldn't my dad have been normal, not obsessed with this place? Things would be so different. I almost thought things would be better, but then I never would've met Crane, or Bones.

Was I willing to trade my dad's life for them? I...

No. I wasn't in the business of trading lives.

"I just want to be normal," I muttered, closing my eyes when I felt his hand move to my arm, slowly moving upward until he touched my neck. Crane was being awfully forward, but I didn't mind. Anything to get my mind off the freaky happenstances around here, and that book...

"You're anything but normal," Crane murmured. "I've known you were special before meeting you."

Right. Because he was drawn to me. My eyelids were slow to lift, and I met his stare, suddenly less than six inches away. "How do you know what you feel for me is real? How do you know it isn't just…this place, telling you what to feel?" Maybe both he and Bones wouldn't like me if we weren't in Sleepy Hollow. Maybe, if this was a normal situation, neither of them would look twice at me.

That…wasn't a good thing to think. It made me sadder than I wanted to admit.

"Kat," Crane spoke my name softly, his breath hot on my face. "You might be confused, but I'm not. I know what I feel."

"What do you feel?" I whispered, hating that I needed to know.

Crane gave me a look that sent my insides a tumble. He opened his mouth to say something, but it was at that particular time the door knocked downstairs. He heaved an explosive sigh, pulling himself away from me. "Brom's here," he muttered, leaning on the granite countertop. "Perfect timing, as always."

I coughed, feeling awkward. Crane was usually the awkward one, but now it was all me, baby. Me, mostly because I had the feeling I knew what Crane was about to say. "I'll let him in," I said, stepping away from him and out of the bathroom.

That was five seconds from turning into something intimate, I knew.

Jesus. Things were too complicated around here.

I greeted Bones when I opened the door, my stomach doing somersaults when I saw his fit, muscular body wearing his normal, everyday clothes and not his uniform. Bones looked drop-dead gorgeous no matter what he wore—or didn't wear, I thought, remembering our time in the otherworld.

His blonde hair was slicked to the side, the corners of his eyes crinkling when he saw me. He stepped inside, and I noticed the bags he carried. Bones headed straight for the kitchen, tossing me a dimpled smile. "I brought breakfast," he said, setting the bags on the counter.

A delicious aroma wafted up to my nose, and I inhaled deeply. It'd been forever since I had a real breakfast. Crane was more of a crepe man than anything, but I liked my meals hearty.

"And don't worry," Bones added, "I brought enough for Crane too. Figured it'd be rude to bring breakfast just for you and me." He began to unpack the bags, pulling out a few Styrofoam containers.

Crane bounded into the kitchen the next moment, practically gliding over the floor as he moved in between us. Yes, right between Bones and I, like he was trying to pry us apart. "What's this about rudeness? Whatever it is, I'm sure you're right. You know all about being rude, don't you?"

I elbowed Crane's side, and the man scooted away from me, going to make tea.

Bones tossed a half-assed glare his way, saying, "Make some coffee, will you? I can't take that tea stuff." Crane looked like he was about to drop dead from a heart attack at that, and they exchanged icy stares.

All the while I slid into a barstool along the island, holding back my laughter. These two...what was I going to do with them? Don't get me wrong, there were a lot of things I wanted to do with them both, but in the long run? In the long run I...fuck. In the long run I was screwed.

People didn't settle down in threesomes. Not really, not usually. I couldn't have them both, even if I wanted them both. Life would not let me have them, and that was assuming I got out of this alive.

Bones set one of the to-go containers before me, and his hand was back in the bag, trying to find something else. "I don't think they packed me any silverware."

"Then I guess I shall be the gentleman here," Crane said, pausing in his tea-making to pull me out a fork from the silverware drawer. "Do you need a knife as well?"

I opened my container and spotted a nice stack of French toast. Holy shit. I hadn't had French toast in years. It was my go-to breakfast during the summers. Loaded with butter and powdered sugar, and these bad boys were heaven on earth.

Since I was too busy eyeing up my food, Bones said, "Yes, she'll need a knife too."

Crane handed one to me, and within ten minutes, we were silently eating. Crane sat to my left, Bones on my right, and even though the two men hated each other, I couldn't help but smile to myself. Nestled between them, it somehow felt right, as if this was always where I was meant to be.

Stupid, because even the original Katrina Van Tassel chose one.

The French toast was gone far too fast. If I could rewind time just to eat it again, I so would. There were few things better than food in the world—sleep and sex were two of them, but that was about it. Once we were finished eating, we made our way up to the library.

It was not the first time Bones had entered the library room in Crane's house, but nonetheless, he had his hands on his hips as he inspected the bookcases along the wall. "I still can't get over how many books you have," he muttered.

"Acquired over a lifetime," Crane said, returning to his desk, his chosen seat when we were in old-fashioned research mode. I always sat near the chair by the large windows—these windows were too large to open, luckily, so no strange occurrences like this morning. That left Bones to sit on the floor, or try to squeeze in beside me, which Crane never particularly liked.

"If I had all the money in the world," I said, "I'd have my own library, too."

"Full of those sex-filled books you read as a kid," Bones chuckled.

"What?" Crane glanced at me, shocked at my younger self's choice of reading material.

I shot Bones a look. "Hey, I had my sex-filled books, you had your Playboys."

Crane's cheeks turned pink as he looked between us. "Oh, dear. I did not need to hear that, I assure you." He reached for his glasses, taking them off to wipe them with the bottom fabric of his shirt. A gesture he often did when uncomfortable.

Such a prude.

Bones would not let it go. He turned his dimpled grin to Crane, saying, "Come on, Crane. I bet you had some inappropriate stuff when you were younger, too. What was it? Did you fall down the rabbit hole of porn?"

Crane's skin flashed an even deeper pink, and he hurriedly put on his glasses to meet Bones's stare from across the room. "I most certainly did not," he shot back, sounding annoyed and an ungodly type of embarrassed.

Letting out a skeptical noise, Bones moved beside me, whispering in a loud voice—so loud that Crane could definitely hear him— "That would be a yes to the porn, I bet."

I giggled, and Crane turned his glare to me. "You do not find this funny, do you? It's crass—"

"Might be crass," I said, grinning, "but still funny."

We continued like that for a while, Bones making funny comments, me trying not to laugh and failing immediately, and Crane doing his best to ignore us and get his full research mode on, for hours. It was the same thing we did every day, ever since being cooped up in this house. Going through books page by page took time, and there was no telling we'd even figure anything out.

We knew the spirits wanted me, but we didn't know what they wanted me for. Bending me over a rock and decapitating me wasn't enough to open the veil. A spell had to be included, and according to Crane, if we could figure out the spell, we could also figure out ways to counteract it.

Sounded easy enough, right?

As it turned out, Googling things was so much easier. A pity none of these books had online copies.

It was well after our lunch break that Bones leaned back on the side of the chair I sat in. He was on the floor, his legs sprawled out before him, his wide shoulders slumped. "My eyes feel like they're going to fall out," he muttered. This was his first full day of research with us. To that I could only say: *I know.*

Oh, wait. *I know* and *Try being the one the spirits are after.* So two things.

"You could always leave," Crane suggested, a note of hope in his voice. If Bones agreed to leave, I was pretty sure he'd leap up and do a dance on top of his desk. Seriously. The man would be that happy.

I heard a rumble come from Bones's chest and knew he was about to say something mean and snarky back, so I sat up, swung my legs off the chair, and asked, "Why do you guys hate each other so much?"

Both men were quiet.

"Seriously, why? You've both warned me against the other, and honestly, as a third-person party in the middle of this feud, I don't understand it." It was kind of funny to watch their bickering, but not constantly. If it was constant, it was tiring. "Is it because of your ancestors?"

I pointed to Crane. "Do you hate Bones because Abraham got the girl? Do you think he's going to automatically claim me like some prized horse?" Next I jostled Bones's shoulder; Bones turned his head, staring at me with warm, blue eyes. "And you," I said, "do you hate Crane because you're worried that, for once, he'll get the girl? Is your feud literally all about me and what happened centuries ago, or is there a real reason you guys hate each other?"

Silence overtook the room. It was not an overly sweet sound. Now was not the time for them to remain silent; now was the time for them to admit what jerks they were being toward each other. Was it that hard? Were their egos that large?

"I'm not a prize," I told them. "You don't automatically get me because Abraham did way back when, and you—" I glanced to Crane. "—don't get me because this is a second chance for a Crane to win. We are our own people with our own feelings. Don't you guys understand that?"

I let out a muffled sound, running a hand through my hair. "I like you both, but not if you're going to act like bickering children all the time. I mean, I can handle some teasing, but constantly? Aren't you guys better than that?"

Bones got to his knees before me while Crane got up from his desk. Bones took my hand, his strong fingers curling around mine. "Kat," he said. "I don't think that. I never once thought that I'd automatically get you. I just…" He paused, glancing to Crane, who now stood near us.

Crane's jade eyes spotted the way Bones held onto my hand, and before the tall man could say anything, I extended my free arm toward him. He measuredly took my other hand, moving to sit on the edge of the chair beside me, his ass barely on the cushion. He held my hand much lighter and softer than Bones did; he was less sure of himself.

Cranes never won.

"We are…" Crane trailed off, his gaze on my hand, which rested on his lap inside his. "…fundamentally different people."

As I sat there between them, each man holding onto one of my hands, I couldn't have said it quick enough: "No." They both stared at me quizzically. "No, you're not fundamentally different. You might have different hobbies, you might come from different families, but you're not different. You're the same. You're both kind and generous and…and you both care about me."

I waited for them to argue. I didn't know why I half expected them to argue, because then they'd be arguing against liking me, but neither man did. They both stared at me in their own ways. Bones held a heavy expression, his blue eyes a deeper azure than before, and he was biting the inside of his cheek, as if fighting himself not to smile at me. Crane's expression was serious, but pensive. Out of the two of them, I knew Crane was the one who would question me the most. He never thought he'd get the girl, so why get his hopes up?

Bones squeezed my hand, causing me to meet his stare. "You like us both?" Out of everything I said, *that's* what he chose to focus on? Oh, dear God. Help me. Pray for me not to strangle these guys. They tested my patience at every single opportunity.

"I'm certain she didn't mean—" Crane started, probably about to explain to Bones what he thought I meant, but that was the thing.

I got up, pulled my hands from them both, setting them on my hips as I walked a few steps away before spinning to face them. "No, you know what? I did mean it like that. You both feel drawn to me like fucking magic? Well, here's a bit of news for you: I have feelings for you both, too."

Bones and Crane were slow to glance at each other, though their stares did not remain on one another for long. It was mostly me they stared at. Neither one of them spoke, as if both men didn't know what to say.

"Well?" I asked, "Aren't you guys going to say something?" The silence. Holy fuck, I couldn't take it much longer. If neither of these guys started talking, I might have to leave the room to cool down.

I mean, if they just stared at me like I'd grown a third eye, of course I was going to feel awkward. Of course I was going to regret saying what I did, even if it was true.

Why weren't these two saying something?

I groaned. "I'm going downstairs." I spun, turning to walk out of the library room, and I heard them both get up. The nerve of them. Near the door, I stopped, tossing a deadly glare over my shoulder. "Do not follow me. If you can't respond to me, then clearly you have nothing to say, so please just let me stew for a while in peace."

Bones and Crane glanced at each other, then must've instantly realized they stood too close together, for the next moment they stepped apart. Not wanting to catch cooties from one another, I guess. With them, who knew.

Neither one of them followed me, which was good. If they knew what was good for them, they'd let me calm down in peace. As I walked down the hallway and the stairs, I couldn't help but want to smack myself. What in the ever-loving fuck was I thinking? Telling them that…of course they were going to be gob smacked. Of course they were going to stare at me strangely, wondering if they heard me correctly. I'd just confessed to them both at the same time that I had feelings for them.

One didn't have a two-for-one situation like that every day.

Ugh. Why on earth did I think it was a good idea to go confessing my feelings? Stupid. Stupid, stupid, stupid. Bones and Crane hated each other, some words from me wouldn't be enough to mend whatever bridges were burned between them. How else should they act when told I liked them both? They would want me to choose, expect me to choose between them like I was the freaking bachelorette handing out roses.

But I wasn't the bachelorette. This wasn't a TV show. This was my life, and as messed up as it was, I knew one thing: I didn't want to choose. Choosing was the last thing on my mind.

Chapter Nineteen

I found myself in the kitchen, making some food. There was no better thing to do than stress eat when you're stressed, right? Okay, there might be some healthier options out there, but I didn't give a single shit about what was healthy right now. Being stalked by spirits wasn't too healthy, but here I was anyway.

Sleepy Hollow and healthy didn't belong in the same sentence together…except that one.

I sat on a barstool, a jar of peanut butter on my lap, spoon in hand. Okay, so I wasn't so much making food as just eating whatever was available to me. I drew the spoon slowly from my mouth, getting a nice mouthful of creamy peanut butter. Both Crane and Bones remained upstairs, which was good. I didn't want them to follow me. I wanted to clear my head without looking at either of their attractive, handsome faces and getting sidetracked.

What was I thinking? Hmm. Maybe I wasn't thinking. Maybe I threw caution to the wind because, *hey, I just might die here*. With the threat of my death looming, telling the two men I had feelings for that I liked them suddenly didn't seem too bad, even if they hated each other and only tolerated the other because they were with me.

And then, because things weren't complicated enough for me, my mind thought about someone else. The Headless Horseman. He was a killer, yes, but he'd never outright hurt me. That was no excuse, I was aware, but still. Everything he did, every menacing appearance he'd made—it had all been to try to convince me to help him. No haunting, no trying to murder me. He kept the spirits away when he could. I owed him.

I owed him, and I'd pay him back by helping him find his head.

I was about to shove the spoon back in the peanut butter, but something caught my eye a few feet down the island. Something that I knew for a fact hadn't been there two minutes ago.

The same spell book as this morning, opened to the same page, too.

Getting off the stool, I inched closer to the book, the spoon hanging in my mouth, free of peanut butter. I ran a hand along the old parchment, feeling a kind of sizzling, invisible electricity tingle my fingertips. The book held power, that much I could sense, and it was old, too. Smelled musty.

My eyes scanned the page, and even though I knew I should call for Crane and Bones, I didn't. Eh. Everyone had the right to make a bad decision or two in their life, right?

Hell, I wasn't even sure I could read what was written on the damn page. An old form of English, one I remembered from high school, being forced to read in and not really understanding.

A breeze blew by, and I was thrown from my own mind.

I stood in the center of town…although, strangely, it wasn't the center of town that I knew, that I grew up with. There were no tall buildings, and the road below my feet was made of dirt. All the people walking around me wore old clothes, the kind of clothes actors wore in century pieces. Ye olden days.

The sun was crisp and clear overhead, no milky white haze anywhere to be seen, so I knew without a doubt that I wasn't in the otherworld. This place was somewhere different. This…this was the past.

A group of people stood in the center of the road not too far from me, maybe thirty feet. They huddled together, watching as two men traded words. Insults, from what it sounded like. One man had blonde hair, its lengths slicked back. He wore a light blue coat, white trousers that were only a little dirty, and brown boots that blended in with the dirt road below. The other man had brown hair, brushed backward into a low ponytail. He held his hands behind his back, an aura of refinement about him.

It wasn't the clothes or the hair that startled me though—their faces did, because they were Bones and Crane, stuck in an old time. The original Abraham Van Brunt and Ichabod Crane.

I was not the only one who was a doppelganger, apparently.

The Bones lookalike scoffed, "Your words are pointless, Ichabod. Katrina will not be fooled by your eloquent demeanor, and neither will this town. You should leave." An invitation that did not sound too welcoming, mostly because his voice dripped venom. He didn't sound like the town hero at all.

Ichabod glared. "Your intimidating demeanor will not sway me. I will not leave Sleepy Hollow until I have wed the lovely—"

I rolled my eyes, not wanting to listen to the men go on and on about her. Yeah, she was great. I get it. Amazing and pretty and...standing a few feet behind Ichabod and Abraham. She wore a clean dress, looking quite regal compared to the others around her. She stared squarely at the two men before her, and I was momentarily struck by the weirdness.

I was staring at myself.

Katrina Van Tassel literally was my doppelganger. Knowing it and seeing it for myself, in person, were two totally different things. It was almost as if I stepped into an episode of the Twilight Zone when I wasn't looking. Just too weird, too...

My thought trailed off when I watched Katrina slowly turn her head, gazing off behind her. I followed her field of vision, trying to picture the town. If we were in the center of the small grove that made up Sleepy Hollow...well, theoretically she could be looking anywhere, since I wasn't sure which way was north, but somehow—call it a freaky intuition—I knew just where she was looking.

Even though it was not in sight, even though it was a good ways away, I knew exactly where Katrina's eyes wandered—the bridge. His bridge. The Headless Horseman's bridge drew her attention more than the two attractive men before her.

"Why?" I spoke, utterly confused in every way.

The arguing between Ichabod and Abraham stopped, and through the crowd of onlookers, I was able to watch Katrina's neck turn, ever so slowly, until she gazed right at me.

Yeah, at me. The person who shouldn't even be here. The woman who was out of her own time. Katrina versus Kat 2.0. The look she gave me could kill, even though she was a good distance from me. Her full lips frowned, and in slow motion, she opened her mouth.

The next thing I knew was screeching. My skin burned, and my head throbbed. Inside my skull, my brain threatened to explode. I brought my hands to my head, as if holding the sides of it would stop me from exploding. Tears fell from my eyes, and through it all, my vision turned pink. They were not salty, watery tears. They were tears of blood, of bone-wrenching sorrow and pain.

And I wanted to die.

No. I wanted…

I wanted to fucking *live*, and this woman, this town—it wasn't going to be the final nail in my coffin.

As my will hardened into stone, I closed my eyes, readying myself to sprint toward her and sucker-punch her in the gut. Something, anything. If she could see me, surely I could hurt her? If she was the cause of my pain, I could inflict some right back. I wasn't afraid to get down and dirty, rough and tumble…

But the moment I opened my eyes, I wasn't in old-time Sleepy Hollow anymore. I was back in Crane's house, standing in his kitchen with a pen in my hand and the peanut butter spoon on the floor. I must've walked to the stainless-steel fridge and yanked off the notepad hanging there, because beneath my hand and the pen, the magnetized notepad sat, full of directions. Directions I didn't remember writing.

The big oak tree near the center of town, due west, thirty steps off the road, at the base of an old, fallen tree, six feet down.

My fingers dropped the pen, and I took a step back when I realized the note was not in my own handwriting. It was far too swirly, and in cursive, too. Who the hell wrote in cursive these days? And some of the words…weren't spelled quite right, almost like the note was written in old English, just like the book of shadows.

Which, I pointedly noticed, was gone. Nowhere in sight anymore.

What the hell was going on? What was happening to me? I reached for my face, remember how I'd been crying bloodied tears just moments ago, but my face was free of any tears, salty or not. Almost like none of it had happened, like it was all in my head.

A breeze blew past me, causing me to shiver, a cold creeping over me and settling deep within me. I turned my head, finding that the set of double doors was open, yet again. My eyes returned to the note for only one second before I headed to the doors to close them. Outside, the world had started to turn to dusk, the sky no longer blue, but purple and red. The sun was nearly setting, and yet, as I stood there, my arms outstretched toward the glass doors, a feeling of ice grew.

Cold. I was so cold. Why?

A sharp buzzing sound erupted in my head, and I threw a look over my shoulders, thinking I was somehow back in old Sleepy Hollow with the original Katrina Van Tassel looking like she wanted to rip out my eyes and eat my heart. But there was nothing behind me. Nothing but Crane's expansive, ridiculously expensive house.

I was about to shrug, to shut the glass doors, but then something cold grabbed my wrist, jerking me forward, out of the house. I fell onto the patio, the glass doors still wide open behind me, falling onto my knees so hard the bones felt bruised. I was seconds from leaping up and glancing all around, and then darting back in the house, but pain spread from the back of my skull as something hit it, and the world went black.

The next time I opened my eyes, greeted by a pounding head and cold stonework all around me—a crypt in one of Sleepy Hollow's cemeteries—I wanted to pretend this was a dream.

But it wasn't. It was real, and I sat, face-to-face with the one person I never thought I'd see again.

My dad.

Chapter Twenty – Crane

I couldn't say how long Brom and I sat in the study, but I did know it was a while. The air was thick between us, a certain kind of tension only he and I could understand. We'd never liked each other much. I was a few years older than him, and I was usually away for the summers, so I never encountered him and Kat together. I was obscenely jealous that he got to spend so much time with her growing up, however.

It simply didn't seem fair, not considering everything. I felt for her just as he did; he was just fortunate enough to know her. Me? I had feelings for a girl I'd never met for years, and then feelings for a woman I never thought I'd have the chance to see. Working with her father, a secret part of me always hoped she'd decide to visit, take a short holiday or something, but she never did. It was as if her father didn't exist to her, and the same with Sleepy Hollow.

And me. The same with me.

It wasn't too far of a leap to think that she could never feel anything for me since it was clear being away from Sleepy Hollow hadn't been too difficult for her, but to hear her say she had feelings for me—and, by extension, Brom—made me both relieved and slightly confused.

Relieved to know she could feel for me, confused that she could feel the same way about Brom, someone who was so immensely different from me. Everyone liked Brom. Just like Abraham, Brom was the local hero, the guy everyone knew and liked. Me? Everyone saw me as the weird eccentric who worked with Phil Aleson. It didn't bother me so much what the townies called me, but it did bother me how easily everyone always seemed to fall into Brom's lap, as if he was the golden child of Sleepy Hollow, just as his ancestor was.

Ichabod Crane was the loser in the story. Nobody liked Ichabod, therefore hardly anyone liked me. It wasn't as if I went out of my way to be liked; I preferred to stick to myself, but still. It was annoying.

And hearing Kat liked us both? I wasn't quite sure what to do with that information, how to handle it. I felt drawn to her, and I could only assume Brom felt the same way, so to hear she felt it too was both enlightening, relieving, and aggravating.

I didn't want her to feel for Brom. I wanted her to like me and only me, and I was certain Brom felt the same.

Brom and I were swallowed by silence for a long while. The minutes ticked by, the world outside slowly darkening. I was slow to look at him, wondering what the man was thinking. Similar thoughts as I was?

Brom must've felt my stare, for his blue eyes slowly turned to me. He still sat on the floor, his thick legs spread out, beside the chair I had moved to when I sought to comfort Kat. We were a few feet apart, far too close, considering I disliked the man, and yet neither of us made the first move.

"So," Brom broke the silence of the room, eyeing me up warily. He said nothing else, probably because there was nothing else to say. I didn't know about him, but my mind still reeled a bit.

"So," I echoed, sounding…resigned. If Kat liked the both of us, I knew it was only a matter of time until she no longer liked me. That's just how things went. A Crane would never triumph in Sleepy Hollow. We were destined to lose, to run away with our tails tucked between our legs. The town's golden child always won out in the end.

"Kat likes us both," Brom went on, as if I couldn't remember Kat's words for myself. I could, and I didn't want to. It was only prolonging the inevitable.

"She does."

Brom's stare hardened as he studied my hunched figure on the edge of the chair. "And we don't like each other."

"We don't," I agreed, meeting his eyes. At least we could agree on the facts. At least there was that. I was sure it was more than what could've been said about our ancestors. I highly doubted they ever stopped trying to one-up each other to even have a civil conversation.

It was a moment before Brom said, "I don't think she'll…I don't think she'll choose, like the original Katrina."

"Technically, the original Katrina was forced to choose Abraham simply because Abraham scared Ichabod out of town, using the Headless Horseman as a prank," I muttered, earning myself a deep scowl from him. "But I suspect you're right. I don't know her as well as you do—" God, I hated saying those words. "—however, I can tell she's not a fan of the old stories, or tradition."

"I'm not giving her up, even if she doesn't choose," Brom warned me, and I glanced at him sharply.

"Me either," I stated, doing my best to puff out my chest and seem intimidating. For a man like Brom, it came naturally. He looked like a weight-lifter, packed with muscles and a stature that you wouldn't want to come across in a dark alley at night. Still, I would not back down here. Even if I thought it was a tad hopeless, I would remain in this race for as long as I could.

Kat...I felt for her more than a man should, considering I'd just met her not too long ago, but I couldn't help myself. This town and its spirits, its legends and its hauntings; it was clear Sleepy Hollow itself had magic. How else could I love her before even meeting her? Why else did the thought of being with another woman make me anxious and sick? Yes, as foolish as it was, I loved that woman, and I wasn't going to sit back and let Brom have her.

No. I wasn't going to run from town like my ancestor did. This time, this Crane, he was here to stay.

Silence once again took over the room, and Brom and I sat there, lost in our own thoughts. It was a few minutes before Brom said, "So, that's it, then? Neither of us will give her up, so we'll...both date her?" He spoke slowly and stilted, as if he couldn't believe what he was suggesting.

I could hardly believe him, either.

Both of us date her? Was that something people did?

"I…" It took me a while to find the words to say, and they weren't particularly good ones, either. "I suppose, provided she wants to do that."

"Yes," Brom spoke, "of course." His fingers tapped on his knees, and an air of awkwardness spread between us. If we indeed both went on to date her simultaneously, I had a feeling this awkwardness would become somewhat normal.

It was another long while before I said, "She's been gone quite a while. Should we go to her and apologize?" At this point, I wasn't even certain what we'd be apologizing for, but I'd do anything to not have Kat upset with me.

Brom ran a hand down his face. "Well, she did say not to follow her, but I think when women say that, they really do want you to follow them."

"Ah, and you know this from your vast experience with other women?" I didn't know why, but I wanted him to say yes, to say he'd been with countless of other women before. A man like him wasn't lacking for female attention, but if he felt anything similar to what I did when I thought about other women…well, maybe he wasn't as much of a sleaze as I thought he was.

"Movies," he said. Brom got to his feet, and I slowly followed. I was taller than him, though I was also skinnier than him, so I couldn't lord over my height to him. "And I have dated, just…" He stopped himself, rubbing the back of his neck. "None of them were Kat, so none of them lasted."

I nodded, not saying anything else as I led us out of the study and into the hall. I was the first down the steps, calling out for her, "Kat—" I brought us through the dining area, to the kitchen, where the patio doors were.

They were wide open, the wispy breeze of the nighttime air sifting inside the house, blowing past us. Kat was nowhere in sight.

Brom tried calling her cell phone, but got no answer. He swore.

My legs brought me to the back patio, and I gazed all around, past the manicured bushes and the stonework and the outside furniture. I didn't see her anywhere. Didn't see any sign of a struggle.

Kat wouldn't have walked outside. She knew the house was safe. Unless…unless someone came here and grabbed her, but then why wouldn't she have fought, struggled and screamed? Why wouldn't she have made a scene? The only thing I could think was that whoever it was caught her off-guard while Brom and I were too busy awkwardly bonding upstairs.

"Crane," Brom's voice from inside the house brought me back to reality.

I ignored my wildly thumping heart and the worry coursing through my veins as I found Brom standing near the kitchen island, the notepad that normally hung on the refrigerator in his hands. He turned the notepad to me, and I took it, studying it.

"What is it?" he asked, and I read the note twice, three times, to be sure.

"Directions," I said.

"To where?" Brom asked, tapping the island in nervousness. When I didn't say anything, his hands curled into fists. "We have to find her. If this town kills her, I'll…" He couldn't say what he wanted to, but it didn't matter, because I felt the same.

If Sleepy Hollow killed her, if a spirit got to her and possessed her, I wouldn't be able to live with myself either. I'd go crazy. I'd lose what little sanity I held onto.

I took the note, a peculiar feeling in my gut, tearing it off the notepad as I headed to the front door. Brom followed me, asking where we were going. I only looked at him and said, "You're driving. We'll need to make a pitstop." I got into his car, not even bothering to lock my house. Didn't matter much anyway; the most valuable thing was still missing: Phil's journal.

Brom got into the driver's seat and started the engine. "Where are we going?"

I told him the convenience store, and he knew exactly which one I meant. It was dark by the time we walked inside, past the acne-riddled teenager behind the register, who sat on a stool with his head in his hand, reading some comic book. The teenager didn't even glance at us; we were the only ones here.

I headed straight to the aisle that had the outdoor stuff; being a convenience store, they didn't have a great selection, but any old one would do. Brom studied me, asking me, "What are you—" He froze the moment I reached for the shovel hanging on the rack, then another.

My fingers curled around the shovels, and I met Brom's eyes, knowing, deep down, the man knew what we were about to do.

The note. There was only one place the note could lead. Whoever took Kat didn't leave it; Kat did.

"No," Brom said, following me to the front register, silent as the teenage worker rung me up and I paid. We exited the store, getting into the car. "Tell me we're not doing what I think we're doing."

The shovels resting on my lap, I glanced at him.

"Those directions—" Again, Brom tried to speak, but was unable to finish. I had the feeling by the end of the night, assuming we all emerged from it alive, he'd be speechless numerous more times.

"The head," I said. "Of course, I'm not certain they lead to the head, but we'll find out, won't we?"

"But Kat—"

"I have no idea who took Kat, or where she is. The Horseman will be able to find her." It made sense if I didn't think about it too hard. This could very well be a huge, terrible mistake, or it could be the only way we'd find her.

I prayed we wouldn't be too late.

I opened the note after pulling it from my pocket, directing him where to go.

The big oak tree near the center of town, due west, thirty steps off the road, at the base of an old, fallen tree, six feet down. It wasn't a comprehensive list of directions, but we'd manage.

The center of town mainly consisted of a park-like area with a gazebo. It was where the town's festivals were held. There was more than one tree, but a certain oak tree was the largest. Brom parked his car in the parking spaces near the sidewalk, and we got out. I handed Brom the shovels, focusing on following the directions.

Due west from the big tree took us out of the park, past the shops lining the area. Directly behind the shops, a field sat, and though I hadn't counted my steps, I glanced all around. Houses butted up against the field a ways away, but I knew centuries ago, this area had been nothing but a field.

Perhaps, even, a battlefield where a certain man had lost his head.

Brom peered around me at the note, and he raised an arm, pointing with one of the shovels. "Over there," he said, and I turned to look. Maybe an acre or so out, a great tree had fallen over, split from its stump. It was the only one felled in the area, nature wanting it back. We hurried to it, and Brom handed me a shovel. "Where do we start?"

Honestly, I had no idea where we should begin. The directions weren't that specific, unfortunately for us. We'd have to dig and hope that the head lay somewhere beneath. Six feet down—that was a long way to dig.

I shrugged. "You start over there, I'll start here." We were far enough from the road that no one would see us, unless they themselves chose to walk in this little grove. It was a good thing Brom was a police officer; we could always use his badge if we needed to. Then again, since he wasn't in his uniform, I didn't know whether or not he had his badge on him.

The moon rose in the sky as Brom and I began to dig. Needless to say, Brom was a better digger than I was. He had the muscles, and he was able to heave the shovel into the ground with ease. With me, it took a little more work, a bit more sweat.

I had no idea how much time passed, but I knew every moment that ticked by wasn't good. The longer Kat was with them, whoever, whatever they were, the less likely we'd reach her in time.

I couldn't lose her. I couldn't. I'd only just found her; to let her slip through my fingers so soon would be madness.

Sweat beaded along my brow, and I ignored Brom's progress with his own hole and focused on mine. Digging a hole was a lot of work. I never knew exactly how much until tonight. Minutes ticked by, though I knew those minutes had to add up to at least an hour or two.

The moon was high in the sky, and Brom was climbing out of his first hole, ready to dig the second, when I heaved the shovel into the dirt below, hitting something hard. Brom heard it, and he stopped to look at me. "Root?" he asked, trying not to get his hopes up.

"I don't know," I said, using the shovel to move some of the dirt around the questionable area.

Brom moved over to my hole, offering me his hand. "Let me." I took his hand, and he helped me up and out, dropping himself in. I leaned over, watching him work.

My stomach was in knots. This could either be Kat's saving grace, or we could be dooming the entire town to hell. It might've been selfish, but for Kat I would do anything. I would do anything for that woman; I hoped we got to her in time.

Brom let out a few grunts, and I was just about to ask if he had it when he reached out of the hole, pushing something out. It was still covered in flecks of dirt, but its top was smooth and ivory-colored in the moonlight.

The skull. We found it.

As I grabbed the skull and dusted it off, Brom heaved himself out of the hole, dusting off his pants. "Now what?" he asked, looking at me. "How do we...how do we get it to him?"

I stared at the skull for only a moment. It was sort of funny how normal it looked. Granted, I hadn't seen many bones in my day, but it didn't look like the skull of a spirit. Just a man caught in the wrong place at the wrong time. A man who was now dead, a man who had died so violently, he became something more, cursed to roam the otherworld in constant search of his head.

He wouldn't roam it in search for much longer.

"We go the bridge," I said, "and hope it isn't past midnight."

Brom checked his phone. "It's eleven thirty-nine. We can make it if we hurry." We left the shovels, sprinting back to his car. The roads of Sleepy Hollow were mostly empty. This part of Tarry was ridiculously superstitious, all for good reason.

I held the skull against my chest as Brom drove like a maniac, speeding and breaking quite a few traffic laws. My fingers dusted out the eye sockets, and as I stared down at the head, I couldn't help but be amazed at how perfect it was. Not a single crack in the skull, even with me slamming my shovel against it. Not a single missing tooth. It was almost like the skull had been preserved, like it was waiting for this night for centuries.

In a few minutes, we arrived at the base of the old wooden bridge that no one in town dared cross at midnight. No one recently but Kat. I was the first out of the car, before Brom even had the chance to park it, and I hurried to the center of the bridge, setting the skull down carefully. The night air whipped up a breeze, and I refused to remain on the bridge as the clock struck midnight.

I turned, meeting Brom by his car. He'd pulled off the side of the road and onto the sidewalk and grass, semi out of his car, semi still in, as if he was waiting to hightail it out of here. Too late to change his mind now.

Brom leaned on his open door, glancing at his phone again. "Eleven fifty-eight," he muttered, meeting my stare as I moved to stand beside him. There were no cars nearby, no lights other than the headlights from his vehicle. We were alone here, and never had I felt so out of sorts. "Are you sure this is a good idea?"

"I don't know," I answered honestly, "but it's the only chance we have." The only way we can find where Kat was.

I should never have let her storm downstairs by herself. I should've—

All of my thoughts trailed off when a different kind of breeze blew by. This was a breeze that chilled me to my core, made me want to be sick. This was a breeze full of ominous foreboding, and I knew, staring at the skull thirty feet away, this might be the worst mistake I'd ever made.

Brom was slow to look at his phone once again, his eyes lingering on its flat screen. "Midnight," he said. He needn't have said it though, for the moment midnight struck, the air cooled at least twenty degrees.

The skull on the bridge moved of its own accord, lifting into the air. Brom and I watched in silence as it continued to rise, almost like an invisible hand held onto it, moving slowly to place it where it belonged— onto the Horseman's shoulders.

The skull's back was to us, meaning the Horseman faced the other direction. Which was fine, especially because once the skull reached the precipice of his stature, once it sat between his invisible shoulders, he did not remain invisible any longer.

The Horseman's tall, wide body appeared, tangible and here, no longer in the otherworld. The skull resting on top of his shoulders ignited into bright blue flames, so hot and bright it was near blinding. I squinted, but I could not look away. This was my first time seeing him, witnessing how terrifying he was.

He had to be at least six and a half feet tall, taller than me, and even wider than Brom. A soldier, definitely.

"Holy shit," Brom muttered, reaching for his hip, for his gun, but he wasn't wearing his police belt, and his gun was not on his person. Besides, I didn't think a gun would do much against the creature before us.

Creature. Was he a man? Or was he a spirit? He had physical form, but any spirit could if they were possessing someone. He...he wasn't. This was his body, and he looked so alarmingly real.

The flaming skull head tilted to the side, as if he was cracking his neck. His gloved hands curled into fists, and slowly veins started to form between his shoulder. Cartilage, muscles, and lastly skin and hair. Hair that was black as the night sky above us, as dark as the uniform he wore.

The Headless Horseman was officially headless no more.

Swallowing my nerves, I moved away from the car, stopping before I set a single foot on the bridge. No more fire surrounded his head; he looked like any other man, old uniform aside, at least from the back. It was now or never.

"We found your head," I called out to him, watching as his wide shoulders rose and fell once. Though he was still a good ways away, I swore I could hear him breathe. His breaths were like growls, menacing and rough. "We helped you, but now you have to help us."

The Horseman said nothing; he didn't even turn to face me. He kept breathing, his shoulders moving slowly, deliberately.

"Not us," Brom called out. "Her."

Yes, the Horseman was connected to her; he'd be helping her, and us. Mostly her.

I glanced at Brom for a split-second before returning my gaze to the Horseman, who still hadn't moved an inch. "Kat was taken. We don't know where she is. Help us find her." I closed my eyes, my voice softening, "Help us save her."

Pleading with the Headless Horseman to help us save Kat? I never would've guessed it was where today would end. Or begin, technically, since it was after midnight. Today was a new day. I only hoped Kat was still alive.

A metal ax appeared in his right hand, and his fingers gripped its shaft hard. The ax, though it had appeared out of nothing, seemed to be just as real as he was. It was a large, two-sided ax, one of its blades shimmering in redness, the other wielded a blue edge.

The Horseman turned his head, his chin nearly touching his shoulder as he looked back at us, glaring with eyes as dark as the night sky, blacker than his soul—if he even had a soul. He did not wear the expression of a man who wanted to help.

I stood my ground, even though I really wanted to turn and run. I was a Crane, but I would not run from this, from him. Tonight, I'd face down the Headless Horseman. If I said I wasn't afraid, I'd be a liar—but love made even the most intelligent men into fools. Right now, I had the feeling I was the worst fool of them all.

I just brought a killer into Sleepy Hollow. Any deaths the Horseman dealt from here on out were on me. I might've made a mistake, but I did it for Kat.

I just hoped it was enough.

Chapter Twenty-One – Kat

Nausea crept inside me, threatening to make me upchuck right here and now, on the stone floor. Around me, a windowless crypt stood, blocking out the world outside. The only reason I was able to see was because of the crack in its top stone roof. It was an old crypt, built for someone who had money.

A large stone coffin sat in the center of the crypt, which was no bigger than my bedroom back home. Maybe eight feet by fifteen feet. The door to it was shut, and though a name was carved into the stone behind the coffin, I could only stare at the figure hunching on top of it.

My dad.

But it wasn't my dad.

It was a spirit that wore my dad's face, and his naked body, straight from the hospital morgue. I saw parts of my dad I never wanted to see, along with how the whites of his eyes were yellowed and covered in film. His cheeks were pale and gaunt, his chest caved in. He looked twenty pounds lighter, and when he turned his head, I saw a stitched mark and a bit of shaved hair. A scar lined his chest, and I came to the startling realization that they'd already taken out his organs.

This thing before me wasn't even my dad. It was just a skin suit that was halfway down the road to rot town.

The thing that wore my dad's face cocked its head. It perched on top of the stonework, its knees spread and its hands jittery. "Awake," he said, "finally." His voice sounded like my dad's, but robotic and cold. Still, it was too similar. I had to close my eyes to stop myself from breaking down.

Coming face to face with a spirit wearing your dead dad's body? Not something anyone should have to go through.

I heard a disgusting sound, bare skin moving, and when he asked me "What's the matter?" I had to open my eyes. He knelt before me, a sick, twisted smile gracing his face. "Cat got your tongue?"

"Fuck off," I said, not feeling very spunky right now. I kind of wanted to curl into a ball and cry, because this was just messed up. An epic sort of twisted.

The spirit grabbed me with hands that were as cold as the chilly, stale air around us. Fingers digging into my cheeks, it made me meet his yellowed eyes, eyes that I should never have had to see again. "You're mine now, sad girl," he said, no breath escaping his mouth. "You won't get away this time."

"Then just do it already," I said, spitting on him. The fingers gripping my face held on harder, and I winced as his other hand grabbed my neck. The spirit was a lot stronger than my dad was, and a hell of a lot stronger than the body he wore would suggest. "Open the veil. Do it. End the suspense." It was hard to get out the words, but I managed.

I also saw stars, so there was that.

"Open the veil?" He laughed, releasing me. "Is that what you think this is about? You have it all wrong. We can't open the veil, even with you. That is something only you can do, witch."

I blinked, meeting my dad's dead eyes. "What?" My voice came out raspy. Being choked wasn't too fun.

"It's a witch's spell, silly," he said, grinning a smile full of yellowed teeth. "A spirit can possess a witch, but that does not give the spirit the ability to cast. That comes from your heart, your soul…" He paused, staring at me like he was getting ready to eat me. "Sad, sad girl. Wrong, wrong girl. Do you know why spirits possess?"

I shook my head, even though I didn't want to. Admitting my ignorance to this thing was not something I wanted to do, but then again, neither was being locked in a crypt with it.

"They hunger." He lunged for me, running his hands all over me, too strong for me to fight. "They desire. They want to feel human. But mostly, sad, sad girl, they want a feast. A soul whose body is possessed doesn't make it out of this world. No afterlife, no white light for you." He frowned dramatically, and I responded by lifting a foot and kicking his lower stomach, sending him flying back. Maybe it was because the body was decaying, but the spine cracked on the stone coffin.

So the spirits couldn't use me to open the veil. That was good to know; Crane'll be relieved to hear that, assuming this spirit knew what it was talking about. What was not so good was learning that they were just ravenous fucks who wanted to feast on human souls.

Oh, and the afterlife—apparently that was a thing. My mind reeled.

As the spirit tried righting itself, I darted for the door to the crypt, but a cold hand grabbed me, pulling me back. This time it was the spirit who used its strength to throw me across the crypt. I sailed through the air, as if I weighed nothing, my back landing on the opposite wall, the one with the etched inscriptions.

Abraham Van Brunt, along with an epitaph that was longer than was necessary.

Of course it was his grave. Whose else would it be? Murphy's fucking Law.

Pain shot down my spine, and I found I could hardly move. My back wasn't broken, just really, really fucking sore. I didn't want to get up. But, as it turned out, I didn't need to. The spirit wearing my dad's body moved towards me, wearing a slick, disgusting smile.

"You do look like her," he said. "I thought you'd be stronger, sad girl. Pathetic girl."

The way it spoke of the original Katrina…made me start to wonder if Katrina was more than she was in the old stories. Just a woman caught between two men—or was she something more? A witch?

That book of shadows…was it hers? Everything was more convoluted than I thought, and it was already pretty fucking complicated.

"Why me?" I asked, not really asking the spirit in front of me; it was more of a general question. A *why me, God?* sort of thing.

It shot a hand out, gripping my neck once again, choking off whatever air I hoped to breathe. "Because, even if you're not as strong as her, you'll still feed me until the day your body gives out." The spirit touched its forearm with its free hand, digging a nail into the flesh of the arm holding me back. When the flesh broke apart, there was no blood, only the sounds of skin separating.

I watched even though I shouldn't. I watched even though I knew it would make me sick.

It was digging out a bone, and when it had one in its fingers, it tore it out, a sickening crack reverberating through the crypt, the worst sound I'd ever heard. Still, its hand gripped my neck, my vision fading fast, as if the missing bone in its arm meant nothing. The laws of physics? The laws of nature? Didn't apply to the thing in front of me, I guess.

I was so dead.

The spirit jerked its free hand at the ground, breaking the bone into a sharp point, which it then hovered inches from my face. "Sad girl, are you ready to be mine? The sooner you let me in, the less it'll hurt."

Oh, yeah, sure. Like I was just going to throw open my arms and welcome this crazy bastard inside of me. *Welcome, welcome. Here, would you like a finger sandwich? It contains a piece of my soul. Go on, I made it especially for you.*

No fucking way.

"Do your worst," I told it, not really prepared to be tortured, but what was I going to do? My back ached something fierce, and my neck was already bruising. I could hardly breathe; it was a miracle I was conscious through all the pain. Still, letting this spirit inside of me was the last thing I would do. It would have to cut me up a hell of a lot before I was weak enough to stop denying it.

I had no idea what made me so strong, why it couldn't just pop into me like it'd done to Mike, but I wasn't about to sit there and ponder it. I'd do my damnedest to make this spirit my bitch.

The spirit continued to smile with my dad's rotting face, the stench of the putrid flesh making me gag. Of course, the smell was the least of my worries. My body hurt, and I was all but powerless when it took my left arm, tugged it taut, and then dragged the sharp, broken bone along my forearm.

Even more pain grew, spiraling inside of me, and I bit my lip to keep myself from crying out. My skin split, red oozing out with vigor. It wasn't too deep of a cut, but it was six inches long and as ghastly as an injury could be. And since the spirit had done it on the outside of my arm, I probably wouldn't bleed out. It wasn't like it cut a wrist.

This thing…it wouldn't hurt me too bad. It would keep me as intact as possible, otherwise there'd be no body to jump into. No soul to spend decades devouring slowly.

"Such nice blood," the spirit spoke, its mechanical voice like razors to my ears. Couple that with the fact it sounded like my dad, and I was in hell. This was a painful, excruciating hell, and I was stuck here for the foreseeable future.

Crane and Bones wouldn't be able to find me. I wasn't even sure where I was. It was up to me to get out of this; tonight was not the night to rely on someone else to save me. Then again, I'd never been a huge fan of damsels in distress.

With my uninjured hand, I reached for the piece of broken bone on the ground. I nearly fell over, my spine in agony. The spirit was too enthralled with my blood to stop me. Before it could move, before it could defend itself, I slammed the bone fragment into its chest. The sharp ivory pierced the hollow chest cavity, with a sickening sound, but I should've remembered there was nothing inside the body to stab. No organs, no heart. Nothing inside it was living.

My dad was dead, and I'd just stabbed his body.

Suddenly, it was all too much for me. My eyes pricked with tears as I watched the spirit reach for the bone protruding from its chest, tearing it out. Not a single drop of blood came out, similar to its arm, which was still split wide open, moving as if it wasn't missing a crucial bone.

"Go to hell," I whispered, and it took everything in me to not look away as it grinned.

"Hell," it echoed, dropping the bone to shoot a hand out to me. Its fingers dug into the wound on my arm, beneath the top layer of flesh, and I saw stars of bright suffering. I cried out even though I tried not to. "You're already there, sad girl."

I blinked, and the last thing I saw was the spirit, my dad's shoulders rising and falling with hollow, empty chuckles. And then I was thrown into the one place I shouldn't be, the one place that I couldn't defend myself from the attacking spirit.

The otherworld.

In a flash, in a single blink, the spirit and my dad's possessed body were gone from my sight, and I sat against the wall of the crypt in the hazy otherworld. Alone. Who knew what would be happening to my body on the other side? What if this was all the spirit needed to possess me? This was the absolute worst time to cross over.

This…I realized in horror, this just might be the last few moments of my life. My last conscious thoughts. Would I be self-aware as the spirit controlled me? Would it be like driving in a car as the passenger, unable to steer or do anything?

I stood on wobbly legs, glancing at my arm. No injury there. No cut. And my back didn't hurt. I was okay in the otherworld, but that was little relief considering what my unconscious body was going through on earth. I had to get back, or at the very least find some way to notify Crane and Bones of where I was.

But how?

Chapter Twenty-Two - The Horseman

It had been so long, I'd forgotten what it was like. Having a head, being complete. Not constantly in search of the one thing fate had denied me for centuries. And yet, now that I had it, I was still not whole. How could that be? My head was the only thing I wanted…wasn't it?

When I materialized on that bridge, when I heard the lanky one speak of needing my help, I bristled in anger. Who was he to demand my help? I did not enlist his help to find my head, and yet…yet he brought her up. The one I'd been following. The one who looked remarkably like another woman I had seen centuries ago. The one who told me she would help me, as long as I agreed not to harm anyone else.

I'd pledged myself to her, and I would not let her fall into harm's way.

With my ax in hand, I started walking.

The two men followed me, whispering among themselves as I took them away from the town, to an older part of it. To a place not many went to. The air was crisp and clean, clear even though it was night. It was not something I was used to, breathing in air, feeling it enter my nose and traveling into my lungs. I'd forgotten what it was like to have a head, and everything that encompassed.

In a few minutes, I walked into a cemetery. It was an old place, looking much worse here than it did in the otherworld. In the otherworld, you could still read the names on the stones, could still see the freshly-packed dirt before some of the graves. Such was the oddity of the otherworld: parts of it had followed suit with the real world, new buildings and whatnot, but other parts of it remained the same, untouched, even after so many years had gone by.

"Who do you think took her?" One of the men behind me broke the silence.

The other responded, "I don't know, but if I had to guess, I'd say it was the spirit possessing the lawyer." The second man was the same one who demanded my help; he was fortunate I owed myself to her, otherwise I might've simply ended him right there.

I didn't get a perfect look at him, just threw a quick glance over my shoulder, but from the small bit of him I'd seen, he looked far too much like someone from ages past. Ichabod Crane.

Oh, yes. I'd heard the stories. Everyone blamed the Horseman for what happened to Ichabod, but a few blamed the other man. Abraham. I was not the one who frightened Ichabod from town. That honor was Abraham's. However, I was the one who haunted Abraham and killed him.

Was I proud of the things I'd done? Would I do them over again if given the chance? It was hard to say. It'd been so long since I was human, mortal, that a part of me did not feel things as I would have, as I should have. Morality was one of them. The difference between right and wrong—I did not know where the line lay. It might very well be beneath my feet; I might straddle the line each and every day.

Was I evil? Was a savior? Was I some spirit caught between? I knew this: I was human no longer, even with my head. My ax, the power flowing through me, was all the evidence I needed to know it. My link to her…

I didn't even know her name, but it didn't matter. Names faded with time. Souls were eternal, and I…I was drawn to that soul, even though I knew it wasn't fair to the dozens of other souls that had made the mistake of walking across my bridge at midnight. I'd ended them or sent their minds on fire; what was it that made this one so special? Was it her face?

She looked remarkably like Katrina, almost exactly so.

I brought us to a large stone tomb. The door was shut and blocked, and just when one of the men behind me started to say he could try forcing his way inside, I shot him a glare, stopping him cold. This one…the one with yellow hair, was a spitting image of the man I'd killed in his own bed all those years ago. Another Abraham.

I did not need his help. I did not need them to follow me. They followed of their own accord. I leaned back, lifting a leg. With one hard kick from me and my otherworldly strength, the tomb's door cracked open, revealing the dark, dank insides.

A spirit wearing a dead meat sack of a body had her still form beneath him, a sharp bone fragment in his hand. She was collapsed on the ground, her head to the side, her eyes open and all white.

I did not hesitate.

I rushed inside, and as the spirit turned its decaying face to me, I threw my ax. The searing red end of the double-bladed weapon severed the head from the body, and both thumped to the floor with a sound that I was certain would make any human ill. The sound of rolling flesh did nothing to nauseate me.

The spirit was gone; no spirit could withstand my ax.

My ax landed in the stone wall a few feet away from her motionless figure, and before the others could rush in, I was at her side in a moment, heaving my ax from the wall. I breathed out a large, even breath, closing my eyes.

When I opened my eyes, I was in the otherworld, standing in the same tomb. She was there, too, as was the spirit I just expelled from earth. She was in the corner of the tomb, whispering something under her breath as the spirit approached her.

It was a hideous thing; something that wore no face and had no hair. The rest of its body looked human, but that was it. No clothes. No eyes, no ears. Nothing but a bulbous thing for a head and fingers that were twice the length they should've been.

Again, I did not hesitate. Hesitation was not something I ever had...except when it came to my inexplicable need to touch the woman that was currently cornered by the spirit.

I flipped my ax; instead of using the red-edged side, I would use the other. The other side was lined in blue, fit for the otherworld. I did not often use it, but here, it was necessary. If I used it here, other spirits would know to leave her alone.

She was mine.

She was mine, and I would not let any of these leeching spirits have her.

I drew my ax in the air, bringing down the blue-shimmering blade straight into the spirit's back. Its strange body went limp, and then, in a matter of seconds, it disappeared from sight and from existence altogether, disbursing into fine, sandy particles in the hazy otherworld air. I sluggishly drew my ax and my outstretched arm back, slowly meeting her eyes.

"Holy shit," she muttered, talking about the spirit that was no longer before her. Then her light green eyes rose, meeting my tall figure, and she said again in a different tone of voice, "*Holy shit.*"

My ax vanished and I took a step towards her. Her posture turned rigid, as if she was unsure of me being so close, her breathing catching in the back of her throat, her eyes never having been wider. Even in the otherworld, their color was mesmerizing.

Forcing her to come back to earth would be an adjustment, but I could not leave her here. She had to come back with me, and she had to come back with me now. I reached for her, grabbing her arm before she could pull away, focusing on bringing our minds and our souls back to earth. Or at least her soul. Me? I was unsure if I had one anymore.

Within a few moments, we were on earth, her soul back in her body. Her eyes remained white, and as she blinked, red tears formed in the corners of her eyes. She couldn't see.

The other two men came to us, carefully stepping over the decapitated body. The one who looked like Abraham held his nose as he said, "I should call this in. I don't...I don't know what I'll say, though."

"Maybe it's best not to say anything," the one who was exactly like Ichabod spoke. "I can't think of a logical way to explain this. Anyone who doesn't live in Sleepy Hollow...they won't believe it." He held in a gag.

Meanwhile, as they spoke back and forth about what to do, I simply stared down at her.

Ichabod bent beside me, undoing the buttons on his shirt and taking it off, revealing a smaller white shirt beneath the first. He reached for her, and I let out a growl of a noise, to which he glanced at me from behind his glasses. "I'm only using my shirt to staunch the blood flow," he said. "She'll need stitches, I think, but it doesn't look too deep."

I let him tie his shirt around her elbow, watching as her eyes returned to normal. She blinked once, twice, and then her head fell back, her eyelids fluttering closed, unconscious to the world. To us. To me.

The blonde one spoke, "I got her," but I shot him another glare. He did not bend to pick her up, simply saying, "Okay. Or you got her. That's fine, too." I could tell by his tone he wasn't certain what to think of me, which was more than fine. I wasn't sure what to think of myself.

What was I, now that I had my head?

I knew one thing, though: no spirit was going to get their filthy, greedy hands on her. Never again. Now that I was here, I would never leave her side.

I reached for her, cradling her body to my chest as I stood. She weighed nothing to me, her body so small compared to mine. Her head leaned against my chest, and even with the blood seeping from her eyes, she was the most beautiful creature I'd ever seen.

Yes. I might be a monster. I might be soulless. I might be everything a nightmare entailed, a being with no moral compass and no compassion, but for her? For her I would be anything.

Chapter Twenty-Three – Kat

I woke to a raging headache, and a prickly pain on my arm. My back was bruised and throbbing, but all in all, I was still alive, so there was that. A warm bed sat under me, sheets drawn up to my chest. My arms lay atop the comforter, and as I opened my eyes to view the white ceiling, I let out a soft sigh, momentarily having trouble remembering it all.

I sat up slowly, eyes falling to my arm. Slowly it was coming back to me. I had a six-inch incision on my arm beneath a new bandage. A long cut from a bone in my dad's body. And then, in the otherworld, that thing with no face…

Oh, fuck. I wanted to be sick.

I swung my legs off the bed, measuredly standing. My body was sore like you wouldn't believe, but I was here, still kicking, so I'd call it a win. My feet were bare, and as they touched the floor, I reached for my face, not feeling any crusted blood. No bloodied tears. Crane and Bones must've cleaned me up.

Wait. I was either missing something, or…

My peripherals spotted a huge, towering figure standing in the corner of the room. A man, six and a half feet tall, his body as wide and as intimidating as I remembered it being. The same uniform, the same heavy breathing. The part that was new? The head resting between the shoulders.

A mouth whose lips were drawn into a line, gaunt cheekbones resting above a square, stubble-lined jaw. Black hair so deep in color that the hue was the blackest black I'd ever seen. A nose that was semi-crooked, as if he'd gotten into a lot of scrapes in the past. And his eyes…practically as black as his hair.

He watched me as I studied him, swaying slightly on my feet. I bet he wasn't thinking what I was thinking, though. Something along the lines of: *holy fuck. This is the Headless Horseman? He's a sexy lumberjack of a man, capable of breaking me in half with his pinky. Why the hell does his face have to be so attractive?*

Because he was. He was a tall, dark, and pantie-wetting kind of handsome.

"Uh" was my brilliant way to break the silence. "Stay here," I said, moving to leave the room. I paused near the door, which was cracked open, to look at him. I held out a hand, as if I was talking to a wild animal, "Stay." Or a dog. Not a sexy, pantie-dropping guy who'd killed someone for me.

Yeah. Talk about conflicted feelings.

I headed down the stairs. I was in Crane's house, which wasn't shocking; this place had become another home to me. Crane and Bones were in the kitchen, talking amongst themselves, sounding...sounding like they were almost friends. Acquaintances. Not people who hated each other.

Huh.

Maybe my life and death situation brought them together.

Bones was the first to see me, and he rushed to envelop me in his arms, careful to avoid my bandaged side. His warmth flooded through me, and I exhaled a lungful. Bones's presence always calmed me down.

A minute passed, and when Bones withdrew from me, it was Crane's turn. Hugging Crane was harder, mostly because he was tall, but I pressed my face against his chest and breathed in his cologne scent.

"How are you feeling?" he asked. "How's your arm? I did my best to disinfect it before I stitched it up."

As he released me, I glanced to my bandaged arm. "Honestly, I'm afraid to look," I deadpanned. I was about to mention the towering figure in the bedroom, but I heard footsteps on the stairs and then in the hall, so I turned my head, watching as the Horseman appeared, standing off to the side, watching me.

Me, me, and only me. The man had eyes for no one else. It was as if Crane and Bones weren't even in the room.

"I told you to stay upstairs," I said, watching as he leaned on the wall near the fridge, crossing his arms over his muscular, solid chest. What would he look like naked?

So not what I should be wondering right now.

"He refuses to leave your side," Bones muttered.

"And his head?" I asked, slowly bringing my gaze back to the two men before me. It was beyond hard not to ogle the Horseman. I didn't think I'd ever seen a finer man in my life. No joke. My cheeks heated up when I wondered if he was as impressive below the hood as he was above it.

"We found your directions and followed them," Crane said, his eyes darting to the man in question. "We took the head to the bridge, hoping he'd lead us to you."

I did my best not to think about the spirit that had taken over my dad's body, but it was hard. The smell. The rancid smell was what was going to stick with me for a long time. "What are we going to do about my dad?" I wasn't sure what happened after I passed out and flew into the otherworld, but explaining to a hospital how a body wound up miles away in a crypt was not something I was familiar with.

"We're handling that," Crane said, glancing at Bones, who nodded.

I couldn't get over how buddy-buddy they were being. I didn't detect a smidgen of disdain for each other. They really did look like friends. Or maybe they were just banding together against the Horseman.

"Before the spirit cut me," I explained, closing my eyes as I fought against reliving it, "it said a spirit couldn't open the veil with me. It's something only I can do. It said even if they possess me, they won't be able to do it. The way he was talking…it sounded like I have power, like," I paused, hating what I was about to say, "I'm a witch."

Now I had three pairs of eyes staring at me, none of them saying anything.

"And, not to add onto this mess even more, but—" God, how was I supposed to say this next bit? "—the original Katrina? I think she was a witch too, and I think she didn't care which one of you won." I glanced at the Horseman, feeling my heart do something funny in my chest when I met his stern, black stare. "I think she wanted someone she couldn't have."

This place, I'd been foolish for thinking I'd be able to get away. I couldn't leave Sleepy Hollow. I couldn't leave these guys, and now that the Horseman was here, full, head on his shoulders, I couldn't let him be. I was stuck here, but maybe that wouldn't be such a bad thing.

Sleepy Hollow might be cursed, a place I'd avoided and hated coming to growing up, but it wasn't so bad, evil, murderous spirits aside.

If this was going to be my new life, well…with Crane and Bones by my side—and the Horseman, because at this rate, it looked like I'd never pee or shower alone ever again—I could handle it.

You know what? Yeah. All this spirit stuff. I was getting the hang of it.

Chapter Twenty-Four - Not Kat

The mayor's office had just put in the order for the festival's flowers. I jotted down the number and which types were needed, the same as last year, no surprise there, and headed into the back room. My shop was on the main street of Sleepy Hollow, just near the center gazebo and park, where the festival was always held.

Always. Without fail, because things in this town never changed, even as the years went by.

My grey hair was pulled back in a low ponytail, but when I entered the back room, I pulled out the elastic band, moving to stand before the full-length mirror near the desk. It was a cluttered space, but I always kept a mirror nearby; it helped me to remember who I was, not the old, wrinkly woman I looked to be.

My reflection spoke the truth, although no one else would be able to see it but me. You see, my outer appearance might be that of a sixty-year-old woman, but deep down I was the same. I might be inside a withering, aging body, but my power remained, mostly. This world would not keep me down. I would rise up, and it would be glorious.

Inside the mirror stood a young woman. Pretty, slim, with shiny auburn hair and sparkling green eyes. Full lips that drew every man's attention. I missed looking pretty. When I had that body, it wasn't customary for a woman to turn down a man's affections, especially when she was orphaned and left with her father's money.

I did not want Abraham, and I did not want Ichabod.

I reached a hand to my face, watching as my reflection did the same. I felt old, wrinkled skin instead of the smooth porcelain that was in the mirror. I closed my eyes for only a moment before willing my mind to the otherworld.

It had taken years of practice, but I could do it now without going blind or crying blood. It was a skill my new body would have to learn.

The otherworld met me in a haze of milky white, and it wasn't long before my pet spirit appeared, her white hair like a spiderweb, defying all laws of gravity. Her eyes were vacant, her teeth sharp as knives. I used her to keep watch.

"Thank you for your help, spirit," I told her, shivering when I heard my own voice. I was Katrina Van Tassel, and even time itself could not stop me. "It's nearly time. Once I am in my body again, I will help you find a more permanent residence." I gave her a smile, and she smiled in return, flashing a mouth full of razors.

Soon enough I would claim what was mine.

I returned to earth, moving to the desk near the mirror. I pulled out the top drawer on the right, retrieving something small. A journal. A journal of a madman, although, truth be told, he wasn't so mad after all.

I wondered what Philip Aleson would say if he knew his own work would be the downfall of Sleepy Hollow. I wondered what he would do if he knew the orchestrator of his own murder was going to take his daughter's soul, too. After all, it was mine.

That body was mine. That Horseman was mine. Fate, destiny dictated it; she would have no choice in the matter. Her time drew to a close. When the stars aligned, it would all be over for her, and it would begin anew for me. Kat Aleson had no idea what maelstrom of misery was headed her way.

Thank you for reading! Please think about leaving a review, even if it's a short one. They really make us indie authors happy (and let us know that people are actually reading our work). Twenty words and a star rating—that's all it takes!

My mailing list: http://eepurl.com/dppf_v

Also, I love talking about books (not just mine. Any book. I LOVE books!) in general on my Twitter: www.twitter.com/CandaceWondrak and on Instagram: www.instagram.com/CandaceWondrak

My Facebook Group: Candace's Cult of Captivation where you can get all the updates on new releases!
https://www.facebook.com/groups/234452154135994/

Be on the lookout for book 2, coming soon!

Made in the USA
Middletown, DE
05 December 2019